Stories and Poems

Julio Ortega

San Antonio, Texas
2007

The Art of Reading: Stories and Poems
© 2007 by Julio Ortega

All rights pertaining to individual translations
revert to the translators upon publication.

Cover painting, "Oratory" © 2002 by Andrea Belag.
Courtesy of Mike Weiss Gallery, New York.

First Edition

ISBN-10: 0-916727-36-X
ISBN-13: 978-0-916727-36-9

Wings Press
627 E. Guenther
San Antonio, Texas 78210
Phone/fax: (210) 271-7805

On-line catalogue and ordering:
www.wingspress.com
All Wings Press titles are distributed to the trade by
Independent Publishers Group
www.ipgbook.com

Library of Congress Cataloging-in-Publication Data

Ortega, Julio, 1942-
  The art of reading : stories and poems / Julio Ortega.
     p. cm.
  ISBN 978-0-916727-36-9 (pbk. : alk. paper)
  1. Ortega, Julio, 1942---Translations into English. I. Title.
PQ8498.25.R8A2 2007
862--dc22   2007033344

*Except for fair use in reviews and/or scholarly
considerations, no portion of this book may be
reproduced in any form without the written
permission of the author or the publisher.*

Contents

~ *Part I* ~

Las Papas

Translated by Regina Harrison

He turned on the faucet of the kitchen sink and washed off the knife. As he felt the splashing water, he looked up through the front window and saw the September wind shaking the tender shoots of the trees on his street, the first hint of fall.

He quickly washed the potatoes one by one. Although their coloring was light and serene, they were large and heavy. When he started to peel them, slowly, using the knife precisely and carefully, the child came into the kitchen.

"What are you going to cook?" he asked. He stood there waiting for an answer.

"Chicken *cacciatore*," the man answered, but the boy didn't believe him. He was only six, but he seemed capable of objectively discerning between one chicken recipe and another.

"Wait and see," he promised.

"Is it going to have onions in it?" asked the child.

"Very few," he said.

The child left the kitchen unconvinced.

He finished peeling the potatoes and started to slice them. Through the window he saw the growing brightness of midday. That strong light seemed to paralyze the brilliant foliage on the trees. The inside of the potatoes had the same clean whiteness, and the knife penetrated it, as if slicing through soft clay.

Then he rinsed the onions and cut into them, chopping them up. He glanced at the recipe again and looked for seasonings in the pantry. The child came back in.

"Chicken is really boring," the child said, almost in protest.

"Not this recipe," he said. "It'll be great. You'll see."

"Put a lot of stuff in it," the child recommended.

"It's going to have oregano, pepper, and even some sugar," he said.

The child smiled, approvingly.

He dried the potato slices. The pulp was crisp, almost too white, more like an apple, perhaps. Where did these potatoes come from? Wyoming or Idaho, probably. The potatoes from his country on the other hand, were grittier, with a heavy flavor of the land. There were dark ones, almost royal purple like fruit, and delicate yellow ones, like the yolk of an egg. They say there used to be more than a thousand varieties of potato. Many of them have disappeared forever.

The ones that were lost, had they been less firmly rooted in the soil? Were they more delicate varieties? Maybe they disappeared when control of the cultivated lands was deteriorating. Some people say, and it's probably true, that the loss of even one domesticated plant makes the world a little poorer, as does the destruction of a work of art in a city plundered by invaders. If a history of the lost varieties were written, it might prove that no one would ever have gone hungry.

Boiled, baked, fried, or stewed, the ways of cooking potatoes were a long story in themselves. He remembered what his mother had told him as a child: At harvest time, the largest potatoes would be roasted for everybody, and, in the fire, they would open up – just like flowers. That potato was probably one of the lost varieties, the kind that turned into flowers in the flames.

For a long time he had avoided eating them. Even their name seemed unpleasant to him, *papas*. A sign of the provinces, one more shred of evidence of the meager resources, of underdevelopment – a potato lacked protein and was loaded with carbohydrates. French-fried potatoes seemed more tolerable to him; they were, somehow, in a more neutralized condition.

At first, when he began to care for the child all by himself, he had tried to simplify the ordeal of meals by going out to the corner restaurant. But he soon found that if he tried to cook something it passed the time, and he also amused himself with the child's curiosity.

He picked up the cut slices. There wasn't much more to discover in them. It wasn't necessary to expect anything more of them than the density they already possessed, a crude cleanliness that was the earth's flavor. But that same sense transformed them right there in his hands, a secret flowering, uncovered by him in the kitchen. It was as if he discovered one of the lost varieties of the Andean potato – the one that belonged to him, wondering, at noon.

When the chicken began to fry in the skillet, the boy returned, attracted by its aroma. The man was in the midst of making the salad.

"Where's this food come from?" the child asked, realizing it was a different recipe.

"Peru, he replied.

"Not Italy?" said the child, surprised.

"I'm cooking another recipe now," he explained. "Potatoes come from Peru. You know that, right?"

"Yeah, but I forgot it."

They're really good, and there are all kinds and flavors. Remember mangoes? You really used to like them when we went to see your grandparents."

"I don't remember them either. I only remember the lion in the zoo."

"You don't remember the tree in *Parke de Olivar*?

"Uh-huh. I remember that."

"We're going back there next summer, to visit the whole family."

"What if there's an earthquake?"

The boy went for his Spanish reader and sat down at the kitchen table. He read the resonant names out loud, names that were also like an unfinished history, and the man had to go over to him every once in a while to help explain one thing or another.

He tasted the sauce for the amount of salt, then added a bit of tarragon, whose intense perfume was delightful, and a bit of marjoram, a sweeter aroma.

He noticed how, outside, the light trapped by a tree slipped out from the blackened greenness of the leaves, now spilling onto the grass on the hill where their apartment house stood. The grass, all lit up, became an oblique field, a slope of tame fire seen from the window.

He looked at the child, stuck on a page in his book; and he looked at the leaves of lettuce in his hands, leaves that crackled as they broke off and opened up like tender shoots, beside the faucet of running water.

As if it suddenly came back to him, he understood that he must have been six or seven when his father, probably forty years old, as he was now, used to cook at home on Sundays. His father was always in a good mood as he cooked, boasting beforehand about how good the Chinese recipes were that he had learned in remote *hacienda* in Peru. Maybe his father had made these meals for him, in this always incomplete past, to celebrate the meeting of father and son.

Unfamiliar anxiety, like a question without a subject, grew in him as he understood that he had never properly acknowledged his father's gesture; he had not even understood it. Actually, he had rejected his father's cooking one time, saying that it was too spicy. He must have been about fifteen then, a recent convert devoutly practicing the religion of natural foods, when he left the table with the plate of fish in his hands. He went out to the kitchen to turn on the faucet and quickly wash away the flesh boiled in soy sauce and ginger. His mother came to the kitchen and scolded him for what he had just done, a seemingly harmless act, but from then on an irreparable one. He returned to the table in silence, sullen, but his father didn't appear to be offended. Or did he suspect that one day his son's meal would be refused by his own son when he served it?

The emotion could still wound him, but it could also make him laugh. There was a kind of irony in this repeating to a large extent his father's gestures, as he concocted an unusual flavor in the kitchen. However, like a sigh that only acquires some meaning by turning upon itself, he discovered a symmetry in the repetitions, a symmetry that revealed the agony of emotions not easily understood.

Just like animals that feed their young, we feed ourselves with a promise that food will taste good, he said to himself. We prepare a recipe with painstaking detail so that our children will recognize us in a complete history of flavor.

He must have muttered this out loud because the child looked up.

"What?" the boy asked, "Italian?"

"Peruvian," he corrected. "With a taste of the mountains, a mixture of Indian, Chinese and Spanish."

The child laughed, as if he'd heard a private joke in the sound of the words."

"When we go to Lima, I'll take you around to the restaurants," he promised.

The child broke into laughter again.

"It tastes good," said the child.

"It tastes better than yesterday's," the father said.

He poured some orange juice. The boy kneeled in the chair and ate a bit of everything. He ate more out of curiosity than appetite.

The father felt once again the brief defenselessness that accompanies the act of eating one's own cooking. Behind that flavor, he knew, lurked the raw materials, the separate foods cooked to render them neutral, a secret known only to the cook, who combined ingredients and proportions until something different was presented to the senses. This culinary act could be an adventure, a hunting foray. And the pleasure of creating a transformation must be shared, a kind of brief festival as the eaters decipher the flavors, knowing that an illusion has taken place.

Later, he looked for a potato in the pantry and he held it up against the unfiltered light in the window. It was large, and it fit perfectly in his barely closed hand. He was not surprised that the misshapen form of this swollen tuber adapted to the contour of his hand; he knew the potato adapted to different lands, true to its own internal form, as if it occupied stolen space. The entire history of his people was here, he said to himself, surviving in a territory overrun and pillaged several times, growing in marginal spaces, under siege and waiting.

He left the apartment, went down the stairs and over to the tree on the hillock. It was a perfect day, as if the entire history of daytime were before him. The grass ablaze, standing for all the grass he had ever seen. With both hands, he dug, and the earth opened up to him, cold. He placed the potato there, and he covered it up quickly. Feeling slightly embarrassed, he looked around. He went back up the stairs, wiping his hands, almost running.

The boy was standing at the balcony, waiting for him; he had seen it all.

"A tree's going to grow there!" said the boy, alarmed.

"No," he said soothingly, "potatoes aren't trees. If it grows, it will grow under the ground."

The child did not seem to understand everything, but then suddenly he laughed.

"Nobody will even know it's there," he said, excited by such complicity with his father.

Family Portrait

Translated by Claudia Elliott

That morning of burning sun my father asked me to accompany him to the market.

He had returned home, as he did at the end of every month, after working on his dead parent's farm. He returned carrying a sack of earthy potatoes and baskets of fruits and vegetables. Having sold the harvest, he brought this proof of his skill, which he announced, triumphant, because the old orchards, only yesterday overtaken by weeds, were producing once again. Later his brothers would come to an agreement among themselves about dividing up the land, although before this, before returning to the modest rice business, he lived, as he had in his youth, the pride of his harvests and the fame of his tender wines. No doubt it was because of this affluence, although short-lived, which had awakened in him the alert susceptibility of old impoverished landowners, that the Lima government included him among the members of the port's town council. The new mayor, Jorge Reyna, an old man made rich by buying and selling houses, spoke of the port as "the next emporium of progress," and the daily, *El Santa,* called the councillors "distinguished neighbors." My father had been appointed Inspector of Weights and Measures.

But this morning he took me by the hand to the market in search of fresh fish, pampanos or mackerel were his favorites, and ginger for the Chinese dish he had promised, in a moment of good spirits, to prepare. When he managed his father's sugar mill as a young man, he had learned to prepare several Chinese dishes with the coolies who cut the sugar cane, ran the grinder, and boiled the molasses. One of them, a very old and tiny Chinese man would appear at our doorstep every year's end for some money because the poor man had lost, many years before, an arm in the crusher. My mother would serve him some food in the kitchen while she learned, laughing good-naturedly, which girls had escaped from the valley or what new feuds were brewing in my father's family. I could never look at his mutilated arm covered by the dark sleeve of his shirt, but his taciturn figure seemed to affirm the wound, my father's guilt before this phantom of lost greatness.

We were almost at the end of our expedition, buying a few kilos of sugar, when suddenly my father loudly reprimanded the vendor, a heavyset man burned by the sun of the port, whose scale, according to my father, did not meet regulations. The man responded with a retort, "If you don't want to buy, then don't buy," he exclaimed. I watched my father straighten up, raising his fiery gaze that contained all his pride. The vendor, nevertheless, exaggerated his crude gestures, undermining the indignation of this man who claimed to be offended, and thus superior. "You don't know who you're dealing with," he said, but the vendor, without looking at him, took back the sugar all at once. "Go buy it somewhere else," he declared. I felt humiliated by this man who didn't recognize the anger of a gentleman, but I was even more afraid he would see my feet. I was barefoot, just like the boys who carried boxes in the market. And I felt naked, as if, at that very moment, I were betraying my father's old anger.

But the afternoon that I caught my mother sobbing next to the dusty vine in the courtyard, I realized that the fear that I was vaguely beginning to feel and didn't know how to define was the threat of a revelation. My mother looked at me, and I couldn't flee anymore.

The morning in the market had revived that fear. The shoddy vendor was the threatening part, someone who had known and had lost all reserve. Someone who was surely allied with the one-armed Chinese man because, between the two of them, my father seemed to lose his place. My mother complained of his friends – they gave him the illusion that everything was the same, but even the girls he brought from the valley to help her in the kitchen left quickly, eloping with a fisherman or a market vendor.

I couldn't run away, and she took my hand. Your father, she said, has asked me to give blood to Don Jorge's daugther. The girl is dying in the hospital, she explained, and she needs a transfusion.

I, who had seen my father tremble with rage, now witnessed my mother's brief, hurt shudder. I didn't know what to do. I, too, was shaken, from fear.

That very night, Jorge Reyna and his wife visited the house to greet my mother. They brought her an enormous tethered red rooster as a gift. The woman hugged her, muttering: "My daughter has been saved," she said. My father solemnly filled the wine glasses.

On Sunday she killed the rooster and prepared a magnificent stew with yellow potatoes and red carrots and called us to lunch.

"They say the poor girl looks like me now," she laughed, with a slight tone of pride in her voice, forgiving us.

The Body of the Goddess

Translated by Claudia Elliott

I

Lived, hurt, lost. I had lived, been hurt, having lost.

I repeated these words to myself, playing a little with them, while I considered the idea of abandoning the Cuzco of my youth and tore up the pile of accumulated papers that one has confused with reality. I ripped up, threw out everything I could, relieved by the oblivion that would soon free me.

But it was then that I found the head of the statuette that my father had given me. Hieratic, the pallid ebony head stared at me while its frozen weight penetrated my hand. For years, my father had hopelessly searched for the rest of the figurine and had even tried to construct grotesque substitute bodies, which the head rejected.

Where did it come from? I would have to take it to an antique dealer, find out its age, its origin, and the possibility that its body would reappear. But it was more likely that the body was broken, unrecognizable; searching for it not only seemed absurd but useless.

Nevertheless, here I was, flying to Lima to meet the two men who claimed to possess the pieces that would complete the goddess.

When I placed an anonymous ad in *El Comercio* to announce the search for parts of the female statuette to match the head that was in my possession, I never expected to receive those two replies in my post office box.

I submitted the ad to mock my father, whose zeal to complete the statue through delirious study and humiliating explorations left him exhausted and reticent. A newspaper ad, I convinced myself, was the quickest way of uncovering the ominous secret of this surely infamous goddess. But when I received the two letters I thought they had come from two impostors, perhaps as I myself was, acting out a mystery because they had been unsuccessful in the more serious games of this world. I decided not to respond.

I was certain they were two fakes in search of a greater farce or craziness to justify their loneliness. I saw myself in them, and I suddenly understood that the part of the goddess that corresponded to them surely had also burned their hands. I responded after all.

And now I was going to encounter them at a cheap hotel in the old section of Lima. From the air, everything seemed once again a bad dream, a trick, a sham. In the world down there, there was nothing lost that was mine; and to leave to chance the name of an inherited passion was to really test the form, the ritual, of a lost promise.

My search was more absurd than my loss. Had I been searching, unknowingly, for this improbable body? Why did this head, cut off from my life, broken in mute pieces, obsess my nights? A thousand times, I studied her features until they burned behind my closed eyes. I looked for her in encyclopedias to provide her with a history. I buried my fingernails in her flesh in order to taste her lunar, nocturnal allure.

What would I say to those two strangers who appeared to possess the persecuted body? Wasn't I the victim of a trap, these men fanatics, and this treasure the price of my life?

Once in the airport, I have only to take a taxi and show up at the meeting.

II

"I've come from Cuzco; you've traveled from Cajamarca, and you from Iquitos." That was what I said, later, in the silence, after the noises from the street had calmed down as we sat in our hotel room before the naked goddess, asking ourselves what to do. I said it as if to celebrate our meeting, but the others were still uneasy.

"I didn't plan to come," said Benigno, the one from Iquitos. His misty gaze crossed the room. "But I have fulfilled my obligation," he added, "I have brought my part and I want only to free myself from it."

Alejandro, from Cajamarca, agreed patiently, as if he knew that there was no point in protesting now.

I returned my gaze to the body of the goddess, believing I recognized her. Each one of us had brought a part of this body to Lima: The guy from Iquitos, the torso; the one from Cajamarca, the legs. Now, with the body finally reunited, we did not know what to do.

"Have you looked closely at her features?" asked Benigno, believing he had discovered another clue. We spent the afternoon trying to guess what kind of statue it was, and if it could, in effect, be made of precious material. "Her eyes are almond-shaped!" he exclaimed. "Couldn't she be an Amazonian goddess?"

I had contemplated those eyes long enough to know that she was, rather, a princess of some pre-Inca culture of the Andean Altiplano. She wasn't in any encyclopedia, but she was in my memory.

"No," protested Alejandro, "look closely at the wide torso; the shoulders are raised, the breasts, small."

We remained silent, looking at the breasts. Benigno laughed suddenly, and although his was enough, we also laughed. We returned to the table, bewildered.

"But you haven't said who you think she is," Benigno insinuated mischievously, and Alejandro smiled, agreeing.

"Although you won't believe it," he finally said, "she is a Mochica prostitute. Look, she has protruding lips, like genitals, and look at her hands. See how thick they are? That's how those women in the pottery of Moche look."

His triumphant voice offended me. Who were they, after all? I was in possession of the head, I had put the notice in *El Comercio*, and I had investigated human and sacred iconography. Alejandro thought he knew it all, and Benigno applauded everything with his easy laugh.

"She is a princess of the Lake," I declared angrily, and the others stared at me incredulously. "Don't forget that I am an archeologist – an amateur, I admit – but I have also been a teacher and have had contact with the people of the highlands. I assure you that the girls there still have these features, and I know what I'm saying."

"Although I am neither a doctor nor an educated man," said Alejandro bitterly, "I have been a farmer in my land, and I know that ancient objects are worth more than gold."

"I don't deny it," I replied. "Now that we have reunited the body we can talk business. We will split evenly the proceeds of the sale."

I spoke conclusively, almost with hatred. They remained silent, annoyed.

"It's a shame to have to sell her," said Benigno, and he sighed.

Alejandro, taciturn, mumbled.

Just then the knocks at the door surprised us all.

"Who is it?" shouted Benigno, standing up.

"Your order, sir!" a voice answered from outside.

III

We were still contemplating the statuette, and we spoke for a while before discovering that the three of us had recovered our part of the goddess from our respective fathers, under different circumstances and without any apparent purpose.

Benigno recalled that his father had hidden the dark torso from him; he had to steal it one night of torrential rain, breaking into a cold sweat while he approached the bed where his father was sleeping with a prostitute, and opened the closet where, among false and golden gods, the pallid long-armed torso of the goddess lay.

Alejandro told us something more disturbing. His father had tried to reunite the parts of the idol, and like us now, even traveled to Lima for a supposed meeting with possible partners claiming to possess the rest of the precious body. He never returned from that trip. He died of gunshot wounds in the street, victim of a trap set for the Communists or the Apristas, no one knew for sure. The police attacked a "conspirator's hotel," said the newspapers, and one was killed although the others got away. Alejandro, who was at the time finishing high school in Trujillo, accepted from his mother's hands, along with sorrow, the lower part of the nameless statue. We were not alarmed when Alejandro took from his jacket a pistol that at first seemed useless to me.

"It is clear," said Benigno," that the statue is bewitched. It would be better to get rid of it; we won't even be able to sell it."

"How much would we charge for it?" I asked, rhetorically. "It's obviously priceless."

"Everything has a price," declared Alejandro. "I didn't come from Cajamarca for a woman that doesn't even move. We'll sell it for whatever we can get."

The goddess was acquiring, in front of my eyes, a brilliance that emanated from her reunited body. But I was dreaming: It was only a sand-colored statue of polished forms – hard, yet fragile, like fired clay.

"We can't sell it," I said, without knowing what I was saying. "We have come to Lima, but there are some things that you simply don't sell."

Benigno grunted approvingly while Alejandro avoided me.

"We have achieved what our fathers could not," I continued. "We have reconstructed her body."

"We are the priests of her body!" exclaimed Benigno, raising his glass, challenging Alejandro's gaze.

IV

When the noise in the hall stopped, we knew that they were going to knock on the door. Alejandro took out the pistol and placed it in the middle of the table. He stood up. He was pallid, serene. With both hands, he lifted the legs of the idol and brought them to his mouth.

Benigno, trembling, did the same with the torso.

I tasted the salty flavor of the head and wasn't surprised that its delicate consistency came apart between my teeth like an unknown fruit.

Tears fell as I realized that it was for this we had come: to hide within our own bodies the parts of the ancient goddess, who would return to us the lost blood.

Now it didn't matter if they broke down the door.

Melodrama

Translated by Alfred MacAdam, revised by John Hawkes

The dream

The deranged girl being brought into the plaza to confess her sin is you: I recognize you despite her pallor and the prisoner's uniform she wears because you stare straight ahead with the same sweet lucidity. But who, I ask myself, not understanding my place in that audience, is dragging this girl here to be made an example of? Her expression has the open and tranquil look of truth, but if you reveal me to these people celebrating your agony, I would have to flee. I want to embrace her if only to convince myself that it is not you. But I just cannot do it because your crime involves me, and I do not want to be the proof of disaffection.

I am a witness of this suffering woman, as if she were an unknown part of me. Or perhaps instead, I am the part of reason that she still awaits, like a revelation in a book.

Now I look for your eyes and declare:

You are myself, without me

That statement is the real enigma of my dream. The verb enunciates her, the pronoun reiterates me, but the language excludes me from being able to define her. She, I read, is what I am not in myself; in her I am someone who eludes me. What is to be done with this girl from my youth who got lost looking for herself?

The spectacle of punishment is crueler and mad. Surrounded by triumphant doctors and lawyers she steps onto the platform to confess her guilt. The mob looks for stones, but there are none, and their anachronism is as crude as their resentment. They demand that the wound be opened in public so that the patient will purge her own miserable self. That violence repels me, but I, her secret lover, am here to recognize her, and even if I am ashamed, I can do nothing but attend the events that rush forward with clinical logic.

Events have the irreversible violence of dreams. But she, with her long hair and torn clothing, barefoot and vulnerable, dominates the brutal theater with her ardent life. Seeking with her eyes, she looks at me, and I know she recognizes me as the proof of her sanity. She looks at me with pain and joy and does not understand my silence.

The tale

When I wake up, my first reaction is to phone her. But how can I say I am calling you after all these years to tell you a dream?

It would almost be better to ask if she had dreamed about us as well, so that at least she would laugh and say, "you're trying to share the luxury of guilt, but let me light a cigarette, you wake me up at this hour instead of remembering my birthday and sending me flowers or at least an Italian compact disc." But I am not calling her, I would not know how to tell her a dream in which she appears like some post-Freudian madwoman and I, her lover, as the witness of her high, tumultuous bed. Unless the dream's strategy betrays me by inverting our roles, and I speak to myself through her.

The confession

We finished the way couples finish, divided between tears and laughter. Then she married. Then she divorced. As in a novel, it was then that we got together again. She demanded the stars from me ("the stars, wait, let me see them"), and playing we extinguished them with our hands.

The sequel

She finally enters the defendants' box with the integrity of her youth, impelled by the impatience of the judges and the noise of the Sunday crowd. Paler but more confident, she looks at all of us, resigned to her clinical death, and says: "Only love would save me, even if it is too late." I expect the huge spotlights of yet another chapter of the national melodrama about the couple without a future to share. But from the sentence she spoke I only understood my name.

The filming

Should I abandon her? Or should I overwhelm the enemy, and rescue her? Literature will be my perdition. It's late even for the very idea of first love. How might I interrupt the ceremony (dream, sofa story, operatic chapter), take her by the hand and escape? Such sentimentalism should make me step back. But when irony comes to save me, I resist it: I prefer the inexorable light of remorse.

Everything is purely emotional. But emotion hampers us and makes us awkward. One should allow the tears to speak. May oblivion save us.

The reading

She has forgotten me perfectly; I am the remote lover that each subsequent meeting makes even more alien. I do not know what she is doing here, in control of the story of my life, a story I will have to obey.

Precise and at the same time illegible, broken writing.

Is there anything left for us to say? Does this concern you and me? Something of yours redeems me; something of mine awakes you.

The dialogue

I said: You are me myself.

And you said: Without me.

In oracular language, that would be a question: Who are you? I myself?

And the answer: Without you.

That is: Perhaps you are myself but without my memory, as if you were liberated from time.

Without me you are.

And I, who am I?

A clearer emotion.

After all, perhaps you went with me, and then left me forever. With and without, we are that slight disagreement.

Every time we met you would pass me a little slip of paper with your telephone number on it, remember? First your parents answered, then your husband, and not long ago your daughter. This time I myself answered: She is not here, I said, she has left.

The good-byes

Why don't you leave me in peace? I am not asking you for anything. What more do you want?

One day you wrote to me, desperate, and I answered you immediately. You asked me about yourself, and I convinced you who you were.

Then you turned your back and immediately went to sleep like a girl who returns to the forest.

You are right: There is always another star.

Liberty Day

Translated by Richard A. Gordon, Jr.

Dramatis Personae

BEGGAR 1: Tall, wearing a dark jacket, tennis shoes and a checkered, pleated skirt. He appears ceremonial and incongruent. He is determinedly rummaging through a big garbage can.

BEGGAR 2: Thin, dressed in black leather, wearing dark glasses. He swaggers around, holding out his hand to passersby, whom he examines, amused.

BEGGAR 3: A young black man, well-dressed, shy. He wears very big glasses and carries a bag full of books. He is a reluctant beggar, always thinking about leaving the streets.

BEGGAR WOMAN: A fat woman, her innocent aggressiveness makes her grab passersby by the arm. She doesn't understand the rejection and speaks constantly. She carries a little plastic bag in her hand.

BEGGAR 4: A young mime, face painted like a clown, carrying a huge broom with which he sweeps behind the passersby.

A corner of Metropolis on a summer afternoon.

A couple walks through the group of beggars, eluding them, irritated.

SHE: I don't understand why there's always more of them.

HE: There's always more garbage, dear.

They disappear.

BEGGAR 1: I'm not a beggar. *(Pause.)* I'm a political refugee. *(Pause.)* I'm an internal exile. *(Pause.)* I am an illegal worker. *(Pause.)* I am post-modern de-urbanizer . . . *(he takes a few soda cans from the garbage can and puts them in his trash bag.)* I'm still missing a piece . . . *(At the back of the stage he empties his load of cans; he sits down to continue his work: he laboriously builds a tower of cans.)*

BEGGAR 2 enters cautiously.

BEGGAR 2: Cokey, are you a man or a woman? *(BEGGAR 1 does not respond.)* From the beard you look like a man. But couldn't it be a fake beard?

BEGGAR 1: I'm not a man or a woman.

BEGGAR 2: You're degenerate. I was afraid of that. You can't trust anyone anymore. And what, may I ask, are you doing disguised as a beggar? This is the only true profession left. Who are you?

BEGGAR 1: Who, me?

BEGGAR 2: Yes, you.

BEGGAR 1: No one.

BEGGAR 2: Listen, my good man . . . or woman, don't feign insanity with me. I know who you are . . . *(BEGGAR 1 stops his work and looks at him.)* Well, I suspect . . . You're a coke addict who snorted his brains out and now collects empty coke cans in fit of regression to the baby bottle. Don't you see? As all of you have surely inferred, I am a psychoanalyst, in the guise of a beggar. I have been forced to mask my identity in order to hide from mad patients who have become convinced that I am their father. I swear it.

BEGGAR 1 returns to his work.

BEGGAR 2: My premise is that no one is vocationally a beggar. Thus every beggar is subject to suspicion. What does he conceal? The beggar is the other. But which? Who?

Several people walk by.

BEGGAR 3 *(following a passerby):* Pardon me, sir, would you happen to have any . . .

PASSERBY: I'm in a hurry, and I can't . . .

BEGGAR 3: Oh, I'm sorry, excuse me, forgive me . . . *(He turns to a couple.)* Could you please . . .

THE COUPLE: We don't have any change.

BEGGAR 3: I'm sorry. Pardon me. *(He is exhausted, yet relieved.)*

BEGGAR 2 is in the center, looking out at the audience, gazing upwardly, with an outstretched hand, his body defiant or indifferent, murmuring to himself. Surprisingly, the passerby approaches him to give him some coins.

BEGGAR WOMAN *(taking a frightened woman by the arm):* A few coins please, ma'am, I'm a single mother, I have two children, one of them is sick . . . Look, I'm taking this little bag of my urine to the hospital, don't run away . . .

WOMAN: Let go of me, let go of me, let go . . .

BEGGAR 4 *(entering behind a student):* Don't you have anything to share? No? May God repay you.

The student stops, searches for a coin, and gives it to BEGGAR 4.

BEGGAR 4: God will repay you.

He uses the same strategy with other passerby. Pause.

BEGGAR 3 *(to BEGGAR 1):* Excuse me, sir, can I see your tower?

Silence.

BEGGAR 3: Isn't it a tower?

Silence.

BEGGAR 3: Is it a church?

BEGGAR 2: Cokey thinks of himself as a great architect. He's building an Off-Off Guggenheim. He cultivates ephemeral art, the lumpen post-industrial culture; a notion of the anonymous and priceless artist. Such purity moves me, but it doesn't convince me. *(He laughs alone.)*

BEGGAR 3: Do you also write for *The New York Times*?

BEGGAR WOMAN: Poor thing. I met another one like him, but he wasn't as cracked as this one. He wanted to paint the whole city white. Thought he could erase it that way.

BEGGAR 4: Well, I think our friend here is trying to illustrate through allegorical abuse, the emptiness that follows the great small death consumptions. After consumption, what can affluent society consume? How can it recycle its own satisfaction? Cokey is creating a new market: her wall of empty cans is a monument to the nostalgia of necessity. He could ask for a grant.

Finally BEGGAR 1 finishes his day's work. He looks at his tower from different angles, satisfied, but he is suddenly frustrated, bitter, defeated. He runs to the huge trash bin.

BEGGAR 1: There's something missing . . . What is it? What's missing?

BEGGAR 2: A screw is what you're missing.

BEGGAR 4: He is missing the mother can, the original can. I knew it . . .

BEGGAR WOMAN: Nonsense. He's missing a door, a bridge, a window. Something besides cans.

BEGGAR 3: Excuse me, but I think he's missing is a title for this thing.

BEGGAR 2 *(furious):* Cokey, enough is enough. Explain to me what in the hell you are looking for? Here, I'll give you these coins, they're yours.

BEGGAR 1: It's useless. *(He throws down the coins; the others fight over them. He exits. Pause.)*

BEGGAR 2: That is a dangerous and unstable man. A terrorist who specializes in can bombs. He's building a time bomb. We're going to have to report him to the State Department, the Department of Defense . . . the Immigration police.

ALL: No, no, no, careful, don't do that.

BEGGAR 2: All of you are his accomplices. You're his army. You help him build that statue of anti-liberty. *(The others have backed away from his accusing finger.)*

BEGGAR 1 returns with new objects recovered from the trash.

BEGGAR 4: Like I said. He needed to go beyond the can as a raw material.

BEGGAR WOMAN: No, I disagree. You shouldn't mix genres. It'll distort the purity of his message . . .

BEGGAR 3: But, won't that be dangerous? They could declare it unconstitutional, pornographic, subversive.

BEGGAR WOMAN: No way. The empty can is all that remains of the rebel.

BEGGAR 4: You know, if he turned 'em in, he could get a lot of money for all those cans.

BEGGAR WOMAN: Recycle, never. You shouldn't feed the monster with its own garbage.

BEGGAR 3: Well don't you think there'd be chaos if the can disappeared?

BEGGAR 2: Please. This anarchism is nothing but a throw-back to the sixties. In the garbage our friend finds a can, but that can is simply another garbage can. The garbage can is a pretext for one can to turn into another. Garbage is a floating signifier: same old story. To another bone with that dog, to another Pavlov, or to another dog . . . Sorry, I don't make any sense.

A group of young men with a boom box passes by quickly, dancing acrobatically. The beggars join the dance as they ask for and receive change.

BEGGAR 1: No, that's not it. *(He puts back the things he had brought from the garbage can.)* It's gotta be something else . . . There's still something lacking here . . . what am I missing . . .

A group of women passes by, chattering. They leave a few bags in the trash. BEGGAR 1 runs over and rummages through them. He finds a round mirror, runs back to his monument and tries to use it. The others watch expectantly. The PHILANTHROPIST enters, followed by his chauffeur.

PHILANTROPIST: Hurry up, Bob.

CHAUFFEUR *(to the beggars):* Let's go boys, over here.

BEGGAR 2: Welcome, my dear sir.

BEGGAR WOMAN: Listen, Bob, couldn't you give us a dollar this time? You have to consider inflation.

They line up and the Philanthropist gives each one a coin. He stops in front of BEGGAR 3.

PHILANTHROPIST: Just a moment, Bob. This isn't one of ours.

BEGGAR 3: Please, don't mind me, sir, just go ahead.

CHAUFFEUR: What's up with you, man? You should be ashamed of yourself. Now go on, get out of here.

BEGGAR 3: I'm sorry. It's just that I'm new. I didn't know.

PHILANTHROPIST: I'm sorry, young man, but I only take care of my own beggars. It's not my intention to cure social ills. I simply add my grain of sand.

BEGGAR 2: And eternity is written on a grain of sand.

CHAUFFEUR *(to BEGGAR 3):* Here, take this *(giving him money),* and get your ass out of here.

BEGGAR WOMAN: You are very generous. I wish I could do something for you in return.

PHILANTHROPIST *(obviously nervous or frightened):* No, please, I insist, don't do anything. Just continue with what you do. You're very good at that.

BEGGAR 2: The gentleman needs us. We are the beneficiaries of his humanity. And we play the role well.

PHILANTHROPIST: Of course you do. Now then, until next week, dear friends. Adieu.

Three youths cross the stage with a radio blasting at full volume. They are dancing about, doing a sort of salsa. Everyone joins the dance, asking for, and receiving, change. BEGGAR 4 and BEGGAR 3 are upstage.

BEGGAR 4: Look at all those people passing by. Each one different from the other. Aren't you sick of all this diversity?

BEGGAR 3: What I see are groups, gatherings, hoards, tribes. I'd like to be in one of those groups. To be a part of a mutual common conviction.

BEGGAR 4: Forget it. Why be part of the others? It's not necessary to have a definitive identity, a demonstrative skin, a name of origin, a proposal for destiny. Now we're all different, it's better for us to start looking for something else.

BEGGAR 3: That's easy for you. You paint your face and think it disappears. But it doesn't. That just makes you a part of another group; just another clown. *(He laughs.)* Sorry.

BEGGAR 4: Clowns aren't a group. We're generic, indistinguishable . . . free of rhetoric.

BEGGAR 3: The mask is another commonplace. Soon, it becomes your real face, don't you think?

BEGGAR 4 *(dancing):* I have no history, no father, no mother, no name or country. I am one disguise within another.

BEGGAR 3: *(imitating him):* Well then, I'll be your mirror, your ghost.

BEGGAR 4 *(painting him)*: You're already part of a group, even if you don't have a name.

BEGGAR 3: What a relief! This mask, this skin, this bone.

BEGGAR 4: You are the best disguise of nothing, or, if you prefer, of everything. Welcome to the end of the nation.

They leave pirouetting. BEGGAR 2 and BEGGAR WOMAN, upstage.

BEGGAR 2: Would you throw away that disgusting bag?

BEGGAR WOMAN: But, I have to take my urine to the hospital for an analysis . . .

BEGGAR 2: No one believes that.

BEGGAR WOMAN: I don't understand.

BEGGAR 2: Beggars used to drug their children to get sympathy. In India there are people who maim their children to guarantee them pity. In Peru, children are closer to death than the elderly. But those pathetic tricks produce the opposite effect.

BEGGAR WOMAN: But everyone has their own plastic bag.

BEGGAR 2: Well, one thing is true: each of us will have to enter his own bag.

BEGGAR WOMAN: What kind of beggar are you, anyway? Do you have to always be complaining about everything?

BEGGAR 2: I am not complaining, I'm protesting.

BEGGAR WOMAN: At this point? Here? Now? Well then, you must be a survivor. You wear your heart on your sleeve. What a beautiful thing.

BEGGAR 2: It's clear the street was made for you. You're probably the only true beggar.

BEGGAR WOMAN: And what, are you faking it? You say you used to be a successful psychiatrist. Seems believable.

BEGGAR 2: Successful, no. And there's no reason to believe me.

BEGGAR WOMAN: Me, I take turns with my husband doing this. It's hard for him to sit around doing nothing. He hates taking handouts. But he always gets more than me.

Two policemen enter and stop in front of the tower of cans on which BEGGAR 1 continues to work with the occasional help of the others.

POLICEMAN 1: This calls for an explanation.

POLICEMAN 2: Yeah, and a better one than last time, which didn't do you much good.

BEGGAR 2: It's self-explanatory.

BEGGAR 3: It's just a tower of cans, that's all.

BEGGAR 4: A modern sculpture. An homage to our city from those of us who don't have a city. A monument to the heroes of our time, the Homeless.

POLICEMAN 1: Cut the crap.

POLICEMAN 2: We could write you up for this. It's against city ordinance to accumulate garbage in the street.

POLICEMAN 1: You're going to have to move this someplace else.

POLICEMAN 2: Hey, you know, you could make a bundle if you recycle that.

BEGGAR 1: Look, I'm almost done. Just a few more pieces and it'll be . . . complete? Finished?

BEGGAR 2: Gentlemen, what you have before you is a struggling artist in a state of crisis. And this piece, it's his only vehicle for expression, albeit ephemeral. We promise to carry every bit of it to the trash.

POLICEMAN 1: There are people who draw pictures on the sidewalk with colored chalk. Some even do it with their feet. That's fine. But this! This is an attack on our sense of order and cleanliness; it goes against our values.

POLICEMAN 2: Not to mention public hygiene.

POLICEMAN 1: And the free movement of pedestrians.

POLICEMAN 2: A bad temptation for their dogs.

BEGGAR 1: All I'm asking for is a few more hours to find the missing piece and finish my work.

BEGGAR 4: We'll help him, so he finishes soon.

BEGGAR WOMAN: It won't block the way. It'll be a very light tower and afterwards it'll all be gone.

POLICEMAN 1: Okay, fine, but what in the hell is it all about, anyway?

POLICEMAN 2: It'd be better if you confessed.

BEGGAR 1: It's a puzzle. That's all.

BEGGAR 3: Ooo! I love puzzles!

BEGGAR 4: But if it's a puzzle, you have to know what it's supposed to look like.

BEGGAR WOMAN: And then you have to know what pieces are missing.

Some passersby stop to look at the tower.

PASSERBY 1: Wouldn't it be cool to knock that wall down.

PASSERBY 2: Yeah, a wall of cans, check it out.

PASSERBY 3: The wall of libations.

PASSERBY 4: The Great Wall, what a joke.

PASSERBY 5: Hey, I'll give you five bucks if you'll let me kick down your tower.

PASSERBY 1: I'll give you ten.

BEGGAR 2: Who will give more? One kick makes for one less wall, use your good conscience, accept the consequences of your ideas. Who offers more?

POLICEMAN 1: No one's going to kick anything, understand?

POLICEMAN 2: This is already becoming a problem.

BEGGAR 1: Gentleman, calm down, please. I need help to complete this puzzle. The pieces we need are in the garbage, or they're on their way to the garbage. There's no time to lose. Please, just help me look. First check your pockets . . .

BEGGAR 3: Here, I'll give you my hat. I think I see a head in there somewhere. You can put it on top of that.

BEGGAR 4: What about my umbrella?

PASSERBY 1: Maybe this book would help, at least a few pages . . .

PASSERBY 2: If you want a tie . . .

PASSERBY 3: Let me see, I have to find something that works . . . or that doesn't work.

POLICEMAN 1: I could lend you my nightstick for a while.

POLICEMAN 2: And mine, it could be a column.

BEGGAR 1: Everything works, everything is useful . . . careful . . . here, on top, you have to add each little thing delicately . . . please, give me some space . . .

BEGGAR 2: Can I jump on the wall? No? Well, then it's a depressing wall.

POLICEMAN 1: I'll stand at this corner.

POLICMAN 2: And I'll stand at the other one. How's it going?

BEGGAR 3: It's coming together, you can already tell, it's beginning to take shape . . .

BEGGAR 4: I need to find a place for me. Hey, will this be the cornerstone?

BEGGAR WOMAN: You can use me in it, if I can be of any help.

BEGGAR 2: I'll turn it around completely in this direction, and now back in the opposite direction . . . Do you see anything? Any change?

BEGGAR 1: It's almost ready, it doesn't need much, just a bit more . . .

A COUPLE: Well, what if we stand right in the center . . . Like Adam and Eve.

BEGGAR 3: Bravo, yahoo, hurrah. And another cheer.

POLICEMAN 1: I don't see anything yet.

POLICEMAN 2: Don't you think it's about time you finished this?

BEGGAR 1: We're missing somebody else, something else, one more piece. Something's still missing.

BEGGAR WOMAN: As far as I'm concerned, it's finished. It's supposed to be the city.

BEGGAR 3: It's the circus we live in. Yeah! Jump over!

BEGGAR 2: The tower of the other, the enemy; of the lost you, wandering . . .

BEGGAR 4: Now I know what it is. It's a new Statue of Liberty! *(He laughs.)* This one won't last a hundred years.

BEGGAR 1: If it lasts a minute that would be enough. A real liberty.

BEGGAR 4: Of course! That's it! How could I have missed it?

BEGGAR WOMAN *(to BEGGAR 4):* Now what are you laughing about?

BEGGAR 4: Don't you see? We're not begging. We're collecting to finance the construction . . . the construction of . . . of some kind of a. . . . Do you see what I'm saying?

BEGGAR 3: He's right, were the construction committee of the monument to the universal beggar! To the reformed beggar . . . rehabilitated? Readapted? Recycled beggar?

BEGGAR 1: No, that's not it. We're not a committee, and we're not going to be reformed.

BEGGAR 2: But we are in fact in charge of this new statue. Cokey, I offer myself as president of the board of directors.

BEGGAR 1: Enough of this nonsense. Just forget it.

BEGGAR 2: But, master, it is obvious that your art surpasses you. Lift your torch for a day to declare our real gain of nothing.

BEGGAR 1: Leave me alone.

They circle around him.

BEGGAR WOMAN *(to BEGGAR 1):* Mr. Liberty, that's what you are. And in the stead of a torch, you will carry the cross of the cemetery, the prisoner's bars, the garbage bag for all of us.

BEGGAR 2: A crown, we need a crown of thorns.

BEGGAR 1: That's enough. There's not going to be any statue, no liberty, no cross, no crown. There isn't anything or anybody.

BEGGAR WOMAN: That's not very nice.

BEGGAR 1: There will be a minute, just one, and that will be enough. *(Pause.)* I have dreamed of a castle in the eye of the sun. But now I'm waking up and the castle is empty. It's nighttime. And there's no one there.

POLICEMAN 1: The party's over.

POLICEMAN 2: It was good while it lasted.

POLICEMAN 1: Come on, let's get this thing cleaned up.

POLICEMAN 2: Everyone go about their business, now. I'm sure you all have someplace to be.

POLICEMAN 1: The garbage truck should be by soon.

POLICEMAN 2: Be careful. Don't get distracted, now.

(They laugh.)

PASSERBY 1: Can I kick the tower?

BEGGAR 1: No. It's mine. *(He kicks the wall of cans, which falls to the ground amidst hurrahs and applause.)*

POLICEMAN 1 and POLICEMAN 2 *(taking out big garbage bags):* Let's get it all cleaned up now. Come on. Everyone. Let's go.

They collect the cans and the other objects and carry them over to the bags, slowly, as the lights are dimmed. The sound of a garbage truck is heard. The garbage men appear, dark, quick, with big gas masks. They collect the garbage bags and the trash bin. While they work they sing in a deep murmur. The others remain silent, still, hands intertwined across the stage, in a frozen dance.

CURTAIN FALLS SLOWLY

The Library

Translated by Naomi Lindstrom

I have come to believe that in the basement of the National Library in Lima there is a trap door, and under the trap door a lake. But for me to arrive at this visualization entails several previous stages of imagining: A spacious all-white main floor (a man is walking down the marble staircase); a roomy basement full of illegible manuscripts (a man looks at the trapdoor and lifts it up). But it's not really a lake; it's a river that the city doesn't know about.

I know that library well. That's why when I request a book on the main floor, with all its hubbub, I usually take it up to one of the offices on the second floor, with its empty desks where I can read it in peace and quiet. Lately, though, I've been taking notes in my hideout, keeping tabs on the so-called passage of time, checking it by jotting down a word and then watching to catch the insidious movement of the employees. Underneath the powerful wall clock, I would copy down words between two employees, who moved from one word to the other, never suspecting I was using a piece of paper, and their movements, to work out a map.

A map of time, I mean. The clock kept an eye on the employees. The employees moved through the minutes of the open doors. I'd rush to squeeze in a word between them. I'd catch them and get it all down on paper. I know the library is not the home of books, but the distinct moments of men, under the presumption of silence.

I've got it all mapped out:

door

clock

man

woman

word

All the doors lead to the books – but there's one door
that leads to the basement, and my map checked out the
movements of the employees to spot the moment when
they'd fall down the stairs to that other time, hidden by the
massive readers. No doubt the map of the library couldn't
show where that pious place was, because, as we all know,
librarians grow in direct proportion to readers and readers in
direct proportion to libraries. That's why at night in innocent
neighborhoods they put up those buildings that no one
imagines will open their doors for business tomorrow.

I could take a city map and decipher the strategic
intentions of libraries being born, which surely would trace
out a suspicious pattern, an umbilical cord or a wall for the
ghetto of virgin readers. But I don't want to be sucked into
another language, just to stick with the doors and stairways
of the library I'm investigating – stuff that doesn't appear on
the official map. Already I know the doors fake their
symmetry; it's only the optical illusion of the space they
pretend to be opening, but in reality are closing. That's why
a naïve reader supposes that time doesn't come in through
those doors; that the slow, solemn space of the stairs is the
other world of a labyrinth or order.

My map shows up this tradition as a fraud. I know the
books are innumerably written, but I also know they obey
this time that turns upon itself like a beast in a printed
jungle. Maybe that's how I began thinking about a basement,
a trap door, a spring flowing. Time passes through books;

they defy it, but the letters and the sentences get lost in the eyes of the reader who perceives that encounter as a threat. There must be an endless spring flowing in the depths of the building, and the vases full of water in the corridors are just to throw us off the track.

I don't know if the library is a triumph of time, the face that looks at itself, or if it's really the defeat of time, as the behavior of readers would presuppose – the face that doesn't know itself. At any rate, when you close the book, suddenly you think a fire's broken out on one of the floors and for some classic reason you didn't hear the alarm. The books, all together, are faithful to their nature during fires, a violent eruption of history through those sacred doors. That's why the library is really a shipwreck, and also why it's an island with no sea, a lighthouse with no island, a language with no lighthouses or nautical instruments.

If that's so, then maybe my longing for a spring will not be in vain. I admit it's not reasonable, but no library is. Besides, my spring is preceded by light and then by darkness: Movements of imagining that ideogram onto my time-map, highly combustible stuff. But I long for more: A doubt with no subject-matter to it. Because that way, my spring isn't a spring, either, but only the image of thirst; that way, my time-map isn't a map, only the momentary flight of fixed words.

I should have started out with this part and then gone on to the images that emerge in my mind. But it's true that libraries absorb such progressions and I could have fallen into the dazzling error of getting them mixed up with the world. It's better for me to have started in the order libraries reject, because not only are they not the world but they don't exist, they're just mirages of one word multiplied by all the others except one.

A similar conclusion could lead me also to presume that the world doesn't exist, but to assume that would be like founding a whole other library, which is hell enough in itself.

Even more desperately, my map of the destruction of a map leads me to suspect that the library – image of itself – takes on, in its nonexistence, the terrible beauty of its arbitrary forms, that demand several floors and, atrociously, many employees and, painfully, a multitude of credulous readers.

To inhabit that fantastic building in an instant is to know it all at once, with the terrible evidence of realizing you can never call time back, and that knowledge, like space and its doors, pretends to fill up the vacuum of white forms whose language we don't know how to read.

That's why libraries should call themselves something else, under the implacable clock, and you should enter them like a hotel or spa, by secret doors, open possible compartments, contemplate the water endlessly.

The Bad Poetry Bookstore

Translated by Alita Kelley

Entering the Bad Poetry Bookstore through a wide double door puts you directly before a long table of old books; in this distinguished place the most important volumes are not the new ones; after all, there are so many of those that it is enough to weigh the possibilities to know from the start how many must be bad, but time has treated the old editions roughly, turning them into curiosities, with their high-flown style and bibliographies of ghostly names.

The bookstore itself is so elegant, so pristine, it demands special attention, almost reverence, from the astonished readers who enter. I pause at the table of old books, rare old books, and for that reason all the more beautiful.

I gradually become aware of a delicious affectation permeating the bookstore, one typical of bad literature. The bookstore wears it as it would a display of erudition, which is only natural, since such literature is unredeemed by irony or the dictates of good taste. On the other hand, it speaks to the reader directly and reveals the distinctive character that poetry, even bad poetry, always possesses.

I pick up a strange edition, a beautifully printed manuscript from the *fin-de-siècle* Paris. It is not a book, exactly, though it tries to look like one; it seems to be one of those nineteenth-century manuscripts bound in sections between announcements and advertisements for patent medicines, that one must read skipping back and forth, like reading a map. A strange manuscript that I would like to own, but the price is high and I hesitate.

Proceeding towards the huge room where foreign literature is displayed, where each country has its own impressive stand, I come to the French section dedicated to great, minor, and forgotten poets. The English section is organized according to the geographical locality from which the bards hailed. As one might guess, the Italian stand is arranged according to the enormous list of -isms contained in the dictionary. Spain, on the other hand, is represented according to the regional prizes offered and the seasonal floral festivities that accompany them. I am surprised by the American section; it is healthy and flourishing and dedicated to biographical variations on the subject. But there is nothing ironic in the way the displays reveal our worst selves; quite the contrary, a discreet resignation prevails.

Suddenly, I am overcome by a fear that this only seems to be a bookstore; it is, perhaps, a front for a secret society dedicated to the lost cult of poetry, now that nostalgia for truth has become nothing but a distant yearning, a reiterating of a question that I recognize and that one always hopes to find answered in books.

I love Garcilaso's blazing light, John Donne's passion, the burnt-out fire of Baudelaire, Emily Dickinson's clear syllables, but none of them are here, though everything is calling to them, and at the same time pointing out their absence. We are alone in an empty temple where the wild birds of absent poetry fly overhead.

I return to the somewhat isolated shelves dedicated to the Spanish tongue and am startled, sensing a revelation. The slim volumes have settled, one against another; they have assumed weight and are innocent of shame at their modest type, crumbling paper, unlikely titles. They speak with that childish lisp of sincerity that so fascinated Stendhal. The very names of the poets seem to have been selected to be forgotten.

Some reader, some corrupt heir to our end-of-the-world rhetoric, must have set up these shelves, these sections, to test poetry's staying power in our days of worldwide markets, homogeneity, amnesia. I know that an even greater yea-saying hides in the nays, and as I take my leave, I know that Wallace Stevens' unique vision, Zanzotto's arabesques, Celan's undying splendor, René Char's ardor are still contained within the illiterate mass. After all, I tell myself, the heart of a reader is beyond good and evil as it curls at the center of clear, expressive language, like some contented animal. Poor heart, I say, seduced in the moonlight by the sirens' song that promises a long, wandering night of sapphires and daisies.

The Incomplete Work of Edward Garatea

Translated By Alita Kelley

Pierre Menard is probably the most outlandish apocryphal author in the history of literature, a man who decided that, without ever resorting to mere copying, he would write a totally new version of *Don Quixote* in which not one word of the original would be changed. More than a writer, Menard is the epitome of a literary activity first practiced by Borges, which privileges reading as a disseminating force that brings into being all that it touches. Morelli, the author whom Julio Cortázar places as central to *Hopscotch*, on the other hand, aims to write a novel that will stand as the first act of a literature to come, a novel to foster change.

Between Melquíades' rhyming in Sanskrit and the last Aureliano's reading about himself in *One Hundred Years of Solitude*, Gabriel García Márquez achieves narrative simultaneity with the instant of reading, as if reality were no different from storytelling. Carlos Fuentes in *Distant Relations* and Juan Goytisolo in *Landscapes After the Battle* have no need to invent an internal author within the story line to reflect the nature of the narrative act in the text itself. In Alfredo Bryce Echenique's *Exaggerated Life of Martín Romaña* and Julián Ríos's *Larva*, the larger-than-life figures of the autobiographical Martín and the Herr Narrator are also characters in a comic performance, which, at one and the same time, constitutes the actual narration.

Reflecting on these masters of the art of vocal attribution has helped me to write a brief literary biography of Edward Garatea (Austin, 1955–Los Angeles, 1992), a Mexican-American writer who carried his poetic principles to the point of refusing to write a single word.

I shall limit myself to a few jottings about Garatea's literary work, since I still doubt whether academic critics or readers will be prepared to test their indulgence through the intriguing work of this most unusual writer.

Who was Edward Garatea? The first time I visited the University of Texas, invited by Rodolfo Cardona in 1973, the young writer could be found in those Austin cafés where a new pop music was exploring Latin rhythms. Zulfikar Ghose and Lars Gustafsson introduced him to me at the tennis court. I had just read Zulfikar's bright novel set in Brazil, and Lars told me that he was just finishing a novel "so long it seemed Latin American." The somewhat elusive presence of Garatea has almost faded from my memory. I recall him as a very young poet who, having taken Christopher Middleton's course on the symbolist poets at the University of Texas in Austin, and doubting his own poetic voice, apparently decided not to write another word. In consequence, he never published a book, and, to the best of my knowledge, this is the first time that his name has appeared in print. His extra-ordinary radical stance well merits our attention.

Rimbaud opted for silence after exhausting poetry as a mere exercise in writing. Valéry planned to stop writing but kept on doing so, quite fanatically in the long-winded notebooks that he wrote during the secret hours around daybreak. Vallejo made even greater, more rigorous demands on poetry, apparently without ever planning to do so; he was drawn into a street that dead-ended, and it probably cost him his life. But Edward Garatea simply chose not to write. Is he, in fact, a writer at all? How can we call him a writer if he never wrote or published a line?

The last time I encountered Garatea was in New York, in the summer of 1986, when I was doing my research on exile in the public library. One Sunday, with Edith Grossman and John Coleman, we went to Gregory Rabassa's place in the country to discuss a possible multilingual journal that would give writers in exile in the United States a chance to speak out. During coffee, after we had thrown out the idea of founding yet another literary journal, Edward Garatea arrived. He'd brought Gregory a recording of Macho Camacho's "Guaracha," and he left immediately afterward. John told us Garatea was trying to get a scholarship to attend graduate school, but only Yale had accepted him.

A current poetic theory upholds that literature can only be said to exist when it is read; an unpublished text, so to speak, cannot truly be classified as literature and only becomes tenable as such when a reader interprets its linguistic signs. From a pragmatic point of view, Edward Garatea would not exist. He would be a writer whose only text could be his name as written by someone else, thus functioning as a metaphor of the textual void, of the non-written literature that fills a blank space in the periodic catalogues of the Library of Babel.

The last time I visited Rolando Hinojosa-Smith in Austin, he showed me a collection of photos from the early 1980s. He'd found them in the files belonging to our late, much-beloved Ambrose Gordon, and in them I recognized several of our mutual friends, casual, nomadic, and happy. I thought I saw Garatea's slim figure in some of the groups.

"Where can I find something new, alive, and different?" I ask of the academic publications and congresses on English literature. After looking over the program of the permanent MLA convention, I return to the empty session dedicated to the incomplete works of Edward Garatea. The works are priceless. Their purpose is to elevate reading to an act of utmost perfection; in their unwritten pages we breathe once again.

When I was preparing my *Anthology of Latin American Poets,* which received such enthusiastically negative reviews, Guy Davenport asked me, perhaps casting aspersions on my entire undertaking, "Do you intend including Edward Garatea?" He knew Garatea had never published a single poem. I considered the matter and answered: "Yes, he's in, along with the young ones." And anyone who cares to open the book will indeed find him there. Mallarmé, who wished to replace the universe with the Book, could not have imagined the way in which a reluctant poet would refute that world in every anthology to come.

Garatea died in the riots in Los Angeles during the summer of 1992. According to investigations by Elyane Dezon-Jones, a rescue team found Garatea next to a wall on which he had written his name. He had intended putting his signature to the conflagration, Michel Rio told me, with a frisson that revealed the invisible influence of the dead writer's absent writing.

I should also like to stress the need for readers to speak up and insist on the poet's right to a place of refuge; I am very much afraid that Garatea's revolutionary work is going to be put forward for the next international prize for impossible writing. It is almost inevitable that poems and stories attributed to him will start to appear, along with articles based on recollections of unlikely conversations; I roundly condemn them, even before the fact, as so much literary fraud. Robert Coover has promised to denounce as apocryphal any work by Garatea that is "rescued" as post-modernist. I personally have checked with Eliot Weinberger's extensive records and find that Garatea's reputation is nothing short of impeccable: He never published anything whatsoever in a single little magazine. Not even in *Conjuntions,* Forrest Gander assures me.

There is, I repeat, a crying need for a writer who unwrites, for a literature free from canons and canonization. John Hawkes has warned me, however, that fame is not merely an academic misunderstanding; it is also implacable. One of these days I shall be called on, I know, to take part in some MLA celebration honoring the greatest self-effacing poet in the language of exile, and I too will be unable to avoid reading his silence.

A Poem by Edward Garatea

I am sorry not to be able to offer more information about Edward Garatea, the unknown young Mexican-American poet whom I had the pleasure of introducing to the public. Several unpublished poets of Hispanic origin have written to me at Brown to discuss the undeserved reputation which, according to them, I have been building up for Garatea alone, although there are many others just as unknown as he. Daniel Halpern has warned me that I am making a grave mistake: Garatea, he says, is by no means as innocent as I have presented him as being, since he published in California's anarchist ephemera. I choose to believe, however, that his work is perfect, that is to say unwritten, though I am willing to study any poems by Garatea that might be forwarded to me. I shall attempt to ascertain whether they are simply works of literary fraud or if they have been wrongly attributed to him.

I spent this summer searching for any traces that might exist of the obscure poet who studied in a desultory fashion at Austin and Santa Barbara. Mark Strand thinks he remembers one Garatea who liked to be called Ixta in order to call attention to his Mexican origins. In a class dedicated to analyzing Garcilaso's sonnet *"Escrito está en mi alma vuestro gesto"* ("Thy likeness is written in my soul"), one of the students versed in current theory – current at any time, that is – explained that the poet speaks of the influence of scientific and religious discourse as a *fait divers*. Garatea replied spiritedly, Strand recalls, that the poem could mean many different things for different readers, but that, primarily, it revealed a lyric clarity, since that which is written (be it on the soul or on the page) is always a miracle that we can scarcely read at all. I believe Edward Garatea's rare poetic insight can truly be felt in those words.

Roberto Bonazzi has offered to dedicate a page to my discoveries, but it is still too early to make any promises; I hope, however, with the help of my colleagues and more zealous students, to gather new information and materials. Meanwhile, Alfred MacAdam has put me on the track of some mimeographed pamphlets that had been handed out by striking Mexican workers and are now on file in the archives of *Review*. Thanks to Alfred, I have now located Edward Garatea's first published poem in the only issue of a broadside entitled *Calle Roma* (1982); it bears the title "A Poem by Edward Garatea" and reads as follows:

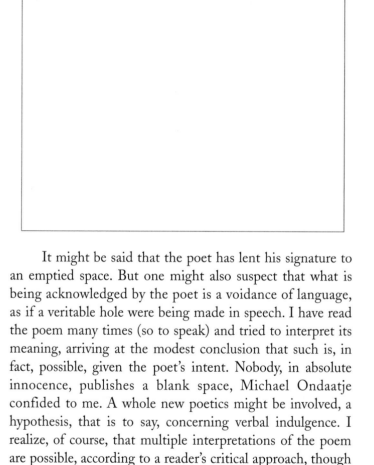

It might be said that the poet has lent his signature to an emptied space. But one might also suspect that what is being acknowledged by the poet is a voidance of language, as if a veritable hole were being made in speech. I have read the poem many times (so to speak) and tried to interpret its meaning, arriving at the modest conclusion that such is, in fact, possible, given the poet's intent. Nobody, in absolute innocence, publishes a blank space, Michael Ondaatje confided to me. A whole new poetics might be involved, a hypothesis, that is to say, concerning verbal indulgence. I realize, of course, that multiple interpretations of the poem are possible, according to a reader's critical approach, though I suspect that a methodology involving philological exegesis (the art of slow reading) or *explication de texte* (the belief that each element suggests another) can shed any light on a text so decontextualized that it is turned inside out. If this poem is not precisely a speech act, it is nonetheless an eloquent act of de-writing. Alastair Reid chooses to consider the text as a palimpsest, which on erasure will expose another poem, most probably by Octavio Paz, beneath it, but I suspect his hypothesis to be somewhat ironical.

Guy Davenport thinks the poem shows the influence of Beckett. The *impronto* of silence, a favorite device of Beckett's, evinces a disbelief in language as common ground, and Garatea, enlightened by this masterly elliptical revelation, must have realized that words do not suffice; his own, therefore, speak silent homage. C.D. Wright suspects the young poet of speaking of the abyss between the plenitude of speech, *parole*, and the mere *écriture* that informs the literary contract. To write a poem, Rosmarie Waldrop adds, is to fall into the abyss, into the open space between the familiar memory of one's own speech and the state-ordained officiality of almost all forgetfulness. Viewed this way, the poem, when it appears on the public page, becomes the voice of a song capable of growing silent in the name of the mother tongue.

Frederic Tuten finds the rhetorical trace of John Ashbery in this text. Ashbery, however, has never dared attempt an act of such open violence; nonetheless, all the elements of Garatea's poem can be found, point by point, in the heterodoxical poetics of *Flow Chart:* The *dédoublement* of the title, the space to be covered, a new form of despair, the missive that is never sent, the appeal to the reader to provide the meaning. Keith Waldrop suspects that the blank space is merely a pause between two letters traveling between two worlds; consequently, the blank is not a codified text that gives pleasure to the reader but a crossroads allowing for the alterity of a new reading.

When Jeffrey Eugenides and Rick Moody visited Brown, we discussed their project of a fictional biography of Garatea. Theirs would be a blank book full of notes. The blank is, in itself, a figure that forms part of the internal geometry of the biography of exile, argued Jeffrey. In the equally elliptical case of Garatea, this might be categorized as a paradox of limits, a decentering circle. Rick added that we could speak of a concave poem, not a hollow one, a poem where language does not disappear but rests while giving birth to a truly American identity, nomadic, post-national, plurilingual.

Susan Sontag believed Garatea to be refuting, with one stroke of the pen, the entire oeuvre of Mario Vargas Llosa. The wretched author of the empty poem was a satirist. Not daring to take on Octavio Paz, whose *Blanco*, viewed in the same textual terms, is already over-read, he has no compunction in facing the Peruvian's massive body of work as if it were indeed the paradigm of every plausible foundation. Nobody writes more than Vargas Llosa, she concluded, and nobody wrote less than Garatea.

Toni Morrison offers a more intriguing interpretation, one that might be considered even problematic: Perhaps Garatea has set himself the task of bearing witness to the first enunciation, articulated, in this case also, as the last. Our first word, which constitutes our first act of learning the mother tongue, is simultaneous with the utterance of our last word. She believes that in this way our bilingual poet bears witness to both the original, edenic state and the final apocalypse of speech in a poem that marries Spanish and English and, by the same act, cancels out both.

I limit myself to offering the opinions of these distinguished readers, while adding that Maureen Ahern has suggested team translation into English as a solution, though Alita Kelley asks if I realize just what rhetorical problems such an enterprise could involve. David Tipton, for his part, believes Welsh would better serve such a borderline undertaking: It lends itself to anti-Aristotelian poetics. After all, Edward Garatea seems to believe in the poetic act as an act of imaginary reader.

A Letter from Guy Davenport

621 Sayre Ave.
Lexington, KY 40505
23 de enero 1995

Querido Julio,

Muchas gracias,
Guy

P.S.   Do you know the enclosed page from Huntington
Cairns's *The Limits of Art* ? An anthology of passages which
critics have specified as the best of their kind. The suggestion
was made back in the 40s that Joyce's last book. "a big book
about the sea" (obviously a continuing influence of Michelet)
be printed, all blank pages.

There are several bibliographies of lost works, beginning with Diogenes Laertius. Shakespeare's "Loves Labours Found" will always bedevil us, along with Byron's autobiography (burned) and that bonfire of mss Catherine Blake made in her yard after Wm's death.

The Gnostic gospels have several places where Jesus imparts information "which may not be written."

And those books alluded to in the Old Testament, perhaps awaiting the archeologist's spade.

Never mind Sappho and Heraclitus.

You have taken *el mernardismo* to the vanishing point – perhaps, always perhaps.

All of Shakespeare's signatures may none of them be his, as it was common for lawyers to "sign" documents, so long as the signatory was a witness.

The Mormons have the "original" papyrus which Joseph Smith translated as *The Pearl of Great Price* – it is a hieroglyphic scroll of one half of a document – the other half is in the Metropolitan, and continues the Mormon half: It is a tax record for some Egyptian department.

JOHN MILTON

MACBETH

Imaginary Works (n.d.)

"The most fascinating poem – certainly, if play it were, the most fascinating play – ever unwritten."

– Arthur Quiller-Couch
Poetry (1914)

The Art of Reading

Translated by Mark Schafer

I

Borges is notified that the son of a friend of his has died. He asks his assistant to compose a message of condolence for him to sign, but the girl cannot find the right words. Borges dictates two lines, but rejects them at once. They don't seem right, he says. I offer to write something less obvious: A Borgesian poem of condolence. True, Borges has never written such a poem, but it is also true that his poetry (like a dictionary) contains all the necessary elements. He likes the idea and, curious, asks me to press on. I write the first stanza: It is direct, clear, it mentions the moon, the father watching the moon, and the night that surrounds him. Later, the poem speaks of the dead son who lies under the trees on the hill, asleep. The lines are nine syllables long. I read and reread the poem and find it to be restrained and enumerative: The tragedy is not stated; the world says it better. But at the end the poem changes. I read it again, memorizing the play of words: Mouth, mute, music. . . . The mute music of the mouth, or even better: Of this world we keep the music of words.

It is no longer a Borgesian poem. I repeat it with my eyes closed before it disappears.

II

That morning in February of 1982, as we were dining in his hotel in Austin, an urgent phone call tracked him from the reception desk to the restaurant. By the cashier, he took the phone, faltering a bit, from the hand of María Kodama. Borges stammered, nodding, but passed the phone to María, who listened dumbfounded: A woman from Texas was demanding that Borges meet her son and read his poems. There was no room for another appointment, but María agreed to a meeting in the airport just before their departure in two days.

III

I went with Borges and María to his old office on the second floor of Batts Hall. The window faced the center of the campus. Borges wished to recognize the places he had been twenty years ago, which in his case was an exercise in remembering. He sat down in the desk chair and tested its comfort, enjoying himself. He ran his right hand, a large and timid hand, over the wood, trying to remember its texture. "It is light," he said, and asked, "What color is it?" María answered sandy gold; I, bright sepia. It is a Platonic object, I said. "An archetype," Borges agreed. The office now belong to a professor of Germanic literature and voluminous tomes of philology filled the shelves. I alerted Borges to this: The books are unquestionably German, I said. "It would be worse if they were irreparably German," he joked, and corrected himself right away, "I owe much to German," and he began to recite a poem by Goethe.

"Light" was a word he found at the time to be just right: Almost everything good was light. Later, he handed me his cane: "See how light it is," he said. But lightness was not just the weight or ease of the object but how adequate its idea or name was. I concluded that lightness is that which words rescue from the indistinct and dramatic density of the world. We were waiting for the photographer from some newspaper and, seeing that the knot of his tie was crooked, I told him and straightened it. The tie was not something light; it was a convention. In the slim Borgesian dictionary, lightness designates the internal texture of things; names are the stuff won from the world. That is why the name of this dictionary of languages is the intelligence of its object.

IV

    That nostalgia of the name itself, of the name as the transparent structure of the entire object, like a classical ear of wheat; that differentiation of the lightest fruits of speech, like flowers alight with their lymphatic tincture; that theory of the weight of things in the balance of language, where values don't come from economy or precision but from identification; they feed the dictionary of the poetry of things, from which springs the thread of memory, the net knotted by speech.

V

The motif of the dead son is absent from Borges' poetry. Perhaps he thought that sons belong to life, not to death, and that a son – as in his own case – is a son forever. As a boy, Borges experienced the extraordinary friendship of his father, who was a sort of theoretical anarchist – or a least Borges preferred to remember him as such. His father's death left him disconcerted, alone in the street of men where the *compadritos,* the fellow of the poor neighborhood, were already characters from a heroic epic of his first stories. That small subworld, patriarchal and oral, was soon replaced by the riddles of time, the arbitrariness of love, the rewritten books. His mother watched over the house and his life almost forever. Soon blindness freed him from the world and honed his language.

On the other hand, Borges was certainly disturbed by the idea of the Golem, whose father, rather than begetting the Golem (copulation, like mirrors, is repugnant because it multiplies men, Borges wrote), thinks it up in an alchemical laboratory, on the hidden page, in Jewish metaphysics. This creature is less than a son and more than a monster: Made without speech, it contradicts the natural order of language and is thus a blasphemous act against law.

Later, Borges dreamed that he was his own son or, rather, the father of himself. Finally, old and repetitive, he met in his dream the young Borges. It seems he was never blind in his dreams, he could see everything again. And he saw himself young again; and the young man saw himself elderly and vaguely unreal. The young man wished to be Borges and Borges wished to be the young man so as to cease being himself. In that instant, on that page, they speak on a bench in a wintry park and know that time is a miracle.

VI

The first thing Charles Whitman did that summer morning in Texas was to kill his mother. He left at once, crazed and armed, and no one suspected a thing when he climbed the thirty floors of the tower at the University of Texas at Austin to the small clock room at the top. Perched there, he overlooked the width and breadth of the campus and a good part of Guadalupe Street. He started firing.

Borges, I've been told, asked to be taken to the tower and took the elevator up to the highest floor. He wanted to feel the time of the assassin heading to his lair. The clock room had been shut by the university authorities, fearing some new local cult, but the tower clock continued musically ringing out the time of day. The pealing of the bells, just like the music, was a recording played through loudspeakers. Before going down, Borges touched the doors and walls of the room with both hands and said: "To think his name was Whitman."

VII

Luis Loayza, in Geneva, took me to visit Calvino High School where Borges had studied during the first years of the First World War. Borges had said that in Geneva no two corners look alike, and that hyperbole was perhaps based on the walk (usually a veritable journey) to the school which stands at an intersection of hills, and might give the impression of one of those baroque streets from German silent movies.

When I told him of taking this walk, Borges came alive and started giving an inventory of Geneva, one of his favorite cities, where he chose to die. He was living in memory, which was not the past but rather the space of a dilated present, he was living in the simultaneous presence of his whole life. I did not, however, tell him that on another visit, I found the Genevan plaza of bordellos where his father brought him one night to initiate him into adult life. His father paid for the services of a prostitute and waited outside the doors. The timid young man was initiated instead into the anguish of sexuality. He lived his entire life in love and there was always a woman close to him. But near the end of his life he came to a stoical conclusion – I haven't been happy, he said.

VIII

Concerning the campus lampposts: These are the only moons Lugones couldn't grasp.

Concerning *One Hundred Years of Solitude:* They tell me it is a novel one hundred years long.

Concerning Professor Merlin, who forgot the keys to an office: How strange, a Merlin who needs a key.

The worst metaphor in Argentine poetry: "Vase with feathers" was what one poet called a canary.

Favorite Buenos Aires street name: *Calle de los Hermanos Jiménez.*

Concerning Walt Whitman: He believed that being happy was his obligation as an American.

The best poet?: Emily Dickinson.

Concerning the success of the Latin American novel: It is incomprehensible, for we have nothing comparable to the Russian novel.

Concerning María Kodama: Her stories of the fantastic are better than mine.

Concerning Joyce: He was a magnificent poet, because of his musicality.

Concerning love: Yes.

Concerning Borges and I: There are too many Borgeses. Perhaps you are speaking with a third or fourth Borges.

IX

The father of *Don Quixote* is not Cervantes, but Pierre Menard, the somewhat extravagant reader who makes his reading into a work of art. The art of reading would thus be that of ascribed paternity: I read this page, I am its maker. Reading, then, doesn't multiply men but books. There are more books than men, more words than objects, more libraries than readers; that is, the world is badly made. It is made in inverse relation to the logic of developments. It forms a redundant figure, an ellipsis in which the I and the you end up finding each in the other.

Pierre Menard is a French "Symbolist," himself a symbol of reading as trans-transcription: To recopy *Don Quixote* is to re-edit it, to discern it, to unread it at random. In that way, *Don Quixote* is inexhaustible. No one has ever read *Don Quixote;* we have read the part of our inscription, that perfect page that bears our name. We are the children of our reading.

Don Quixote, in short, is a book multiplied by all its readers, a Babelic library where mere Spanish is transformed into the tongue of tongues, the spring at which drink the survivors of the desert of the blank page. That is why *Don Quixote* can only be a guide to *Don Quixote,* an abridged edition for children at the quixotic age.

Mother of truth was what Cervantes called history, using a commonplace phrase. Mother of truth was what Menard called it, implying the tragic force of history that reveals us. It is the same text. The mothers are not the same because the sons, the line of La Mancha, are not the same: We are history, its true handwriting.

To Cervantes, his Quixote was "a gaunt, parched, fanciful son, full of a variety of thoughts never imagined by anyone else." Gaunt, full, unique. "To be Alonso Quixano and not dare to be Don Quixote," wrote Borges in 1979.

X

In "Pierre Menard, Author of Don Quixote" one reads that a "philological fragment of Novalis – the one bearing the number 2005 in the Dresden edition – that sketches out the theme of the *total* identification with a specific author" is one of the texts that inspired his undertaking. I bumped into it in Ernesto Volkening's translation of the "Pollen" series published by *Eco* (Bogotá, No. 147, July 1972):

"I show I understand a writer only when I know how to act according to his own understanding, when, without reducing his individuality, I might know how to translate and change him around in a multiplicity of ways."

Novalis literally proposes translation as an activity that substitutes the reader for the author: Becoming the author is the only way of understanding him, and that is demonstrated in the free rewriting of the work of the other, now one's own.

I had another version, which my friend Wolfgang A. Luchting did for me, not without warning me that German is untranslatable into Spanish: "I show that I have understood an author only if I am capable of acting in his spirit; if I can translate him and transform him in many ways without diminishing his individuality."

Here, Novalis is, I believe, closer to Borges. In Volkening's text, the conditional and the future (when I know), the symmetry (understand, understanding) and the single phrase belabor the meaning (when I know, I might know). In my friend's, however, the second phrase illustrates and amplifies the first.

To act in someone's spirit without diminishing his individuality means: Without losing myself in those translations of boundless variations. Translation, evidently, is not just reading. It is reformulation, remaking the text, pursuing it from where its author left it to our (other, own) discourse.

Borges prefers to call this phenomenon of intra-writing "*total* identification with the author," but it's clear that he is stretching the meaning, inasmuch as the individualities don't mingle. The identification is complete but textual.

Menard, in this poetics of the felicitous collaboration with the literary work, rewrites *Don Quixote* without copying it but literally appropriating its words to actualize its meaning. The total reading would thus be the most textual: The de-explication of texts. Reading capable of the greatest faithfulness, that of being other and the same in the other yet same act of reading another page.

XI

Mario Usabiaga passed through Austin shortly after Borges' visit. He had been living in Mexico since he was released from the Argentine military prison where he was held for several years. His life was saved thanks to international protest, and also by a crude fluke of the killing. Torture marked him profoundly: He had glimpsed a horror that few men have managed to speak of. Mario's face was etched with anguish and he spoke with a calm, painful intensity. After the torture sessions, the jailer decided who would die that night. The prisoners knew it, and waited in silence, unreal. They would fall asleep in the exhaustion of waiting. Suddenly the footfalls, the trembling doors, the light in one of the cells. And voices and shouting. Twice they opened the doors to his cell and took away two cellmates. They had anticipated this: The three of them had memorized messages, papers, goodbyes. That solidarity of death made them less mortal. "Tomorrow we will come for you," they told him each of those nights. Finally he was set free, but he was desolated by the horror and fear. He would remember all the days and nights of his imprisonment one by one and in his dreams he was still in prison: He would wake up as if he had glimpsed the exit. As a semiologist, he was obsessed with the discourses of violence, by its technology. What type of sin was torture if the torturer is Catholic? What penance would the Church assign to him in the confessional? Less systematic, no less atrocious, would be the inability of justice to do justice. Did it all begin with the old dichotomy of civilization and barbarism? Based on what ancient negations of the other could this killing have begun?

There weren't answers to so many questions. And his life was running out as he tried to understand it. He died soon after. He left me a few essays he had translated of

Umberto Eco and the letter in which Eco asked the Argentine military to guarantee the life of the young, imprisoned professor.

He also left me an unpublished article on Borges that he signed as Mario García. It was in reality a secret letter to Borges in which he complained of the disagreeable nationalistic praise certain writers (of substance, as Bustos Domecq would say) dedicated to him on the occasion of his having lost, once again, the Nobel Prize for Literature. That utilitarian nationalism ("thanks to the recognition of Borges, the Europeans know that the Argentines are not a bunch of savages we are made out to be by the international campaign") legitimated the dictatorship, denounced Mario García, and reduced Borges to a name manipulated by the military. This letter protested to Borges on behalf of Borges, and ended up as another chapter in the periodic dialogue between "Borges and I."

But the article ended with something unusual: A poem written in slang by an imprisoned *campadrito*. While in prison, Mario translated it into another poem in common Spanish, parallel yet understandable. The *compadrito* had written a refutation of Borges: He reproached him for talking of his fellows without knowing them, and in the only verbal maneuver that Borges could not have made on his own, he wrote the poem in pure slang, in a secret argot that rejected literature to preserve the language of his survival.

"What we have [my friend wrote] is a poem written about twenty years ago [around 1959] in a prison of Córdoba, Argentina, by someone in prison for murder. One of his friends who would visit him in the pen collected these verses by memory, which never had any propagation other than an occasional wine-soaked delivery, very infrequent, by this friend late at night in some bar. "The language of the poem, similar to that of the underworld of Buenos Aires in the early part of this century, remains current today in the jails and on those vague borders between bohemians and marginal people."

As we see here, Mario rewrites both the slang (he poses as a *compadrito*) and Borges' style (through the use of metaphor and adjectives).

The poem is entitled *Pa' Borges:*

> *Te bato de butaca la granzúa*
> *de mirarte chamuyar pulentería,*
> *de chorros, mecheras, taquería*
> *y el buzonear de giles y de púas.*
>
> *Te furqueo sobrador chapando el vuelo*
> *pa' escrachar de tue tálamo de rosas.*
> *Yo en mi fule lunfardear engomo un cielo*
> *bien debute del batir de tantas cosas.*
>
> *Tue verso rebuscado no es la yeca*
> *donde rula la mersa del estaño.*
> *Voz amás al salame sin zabeca*
> *que no manya el rebusque de los caños.*

Por: El gomía de la reja

It is, we shall add, a total rewriting of Borges starting with its use of words: The words tell of reality and our place in it. This argument for language, for the street and its speech, doesn't ignore the work of Borges; on the contrary, it wishes to, so to speak, deborgesize Borges.

Mario Usabiago (Mario García, on transcribing his transcription) offers this "more universal" version:

For Borges

I want to tell you how strange it is
to hear you speak of serious things:
of thieves, pickpockets, the hateful cops,
and all that goes on between the dumb and the quick.

I find you vain, recording jumbled particulars
to concoct false tales from your bed of roses.
I, in my poor slang, embrace a sky
made beautiful by the voice of so many things.

Your obscure verses are not the street
where the night and the real suburbs walk.
You love the hollow men who don't understand
the laws of rogues and the wit
by which so many wretches survive.

By: The friend behind bars

It is certainly a very loose rendering but at the same time a fair one. The tension and edge of the original is lost but it takes on conversation and fable. Rewriting a rewrite of Borges: This manner of reading is already included in the Borgesian hypothesis that we are all a single text, variable, fluid, and perpetual.

Mario understood with lucidity that the poem he held in his hands (it is known that the prisoners stay sane, at times, thanks to a few verses which they cling to as to the edge of language) possessed its own strength far beyond the reading of irony: That power had to do with politics, with what he called "the use of Borges." Not knowing what else to do with the poem, he included it in a note of protest against the nationalism of the hypocritical bourgeoisie. But this note was exceeded by the poem at the end. For if there were many

Borgeses, it was because there were many readers. What the poem demonstrates is that if the bourgeoisie was attempting to possess Borges, the people, in order to claim him, began by rejecting him. This reading demanded his rewriting and was, therefore, more radical.

Carlos Fuentes is right: When someone tells us his life, he is entrusting us with a tale that burns our hands, and all we can do is immediately pass it on.

XII

And what if Mario was in fact the author of that poem written in slang? I would prefer that not be the case, but literature is infinite, in contrast to reality.

The story of that poor prisoner who composes the poem in code, of the friend who visits him in jail and memorizes the text and later repeats it to friends over wine, and, much later, of someone who copies and translates it is – to say the least – the universal history of literature.

It is believable that Mario might have written the poem during his prison years and translated it as an intellectual game to pass the time with his companions. Mario was a semiotician and was interested in the image of Borges then being circulated with antagonistic values; he was a politician and saw the improper use of that image, a cultural loss which he proposed to correct; and he was, above all, a translator (I've lost Umberto Eco's letter but I believe Mario was his student in medieval religious rhetoric in his seminar in Milan). It wouldn't surprise me at all if what he calls the translation of the original he actually retranslated into slang. I suspect that few poets write in slang but I can believe that someone might rewrite a text in that demotic code. Author, translator, critic: Mario multiplied himself to make the voices that speak behind the texts of Borges more genuine. He made Borges father of his creature so that this *compadrito*, upon faithfully contradicting him would release him into unconstrained speech, into the heart of history.

From prison, Mario proposed the freedom of Borges.

XIII

In that slightly sarcastic tone of voice by which Borges subverted his own comments, he had said to me: "This world is excessively written. But there are some pages, a few, that have the texture of time. In the printed jungle, time turns on these pages, on itself, and watches us."

Alfonso Reyes, I said, affirms that "the other *Quixote* must still be written: *The History of the Ingenious Hidalgo Who From So Much Reading Devised Writing.*"

This other Quixote, he laughed, devoured books which are, as Gracián says, "grass of the soul."

Someone asserts, I asserted, that reading is an "escape from time" and that the reader must be suspected of "the secret desire of removing himself from the implacable succession of time that leads to death."

That would be the equivalent then, he said, to dreaming. And I don't know anyone who reads while asleep; although one can't put anything past Lugones. I now remember that I myself have said, as a young man, that one nods through *Ulysses.*

If life is a dream, who reads the book of life? Someone who dreams he is awake? I asked.

I'm going to tell you a sentence that came to me as I woke, not long ago: Imagine an executioner who was able to create a phrase out of strange words which, when uttered, would produce the immediate death of the condemned person.

I recorded the sentence and said, with excessive enthusiasm: There would be a different and unique phrase for each condemned person and his death.

We are all condemned, he smiled, and one word would be enough.

Wallace Stevens, I continued, asked the wind what syllable it was looking for in the distance of the dream.

"Vocalissimus. Say it." The wind is the word of the dream that doesn't speak, he commented.

After a long pause, he added: Attempt, nevertheless, to tell us something. Stammer. Vocalize, try the possible vowels. The wind will say one thing instead of another, right?

You, as a young man, said that writing is doing one thing instead of another, I said, unable to follow him.

I don't remember, he replied. You see, all that awaits us is stuttering, forgetfulness.

I remained silent.

Reading is risky, isn't that true? There is a page I'm still composing in my head; I no longer write and scarcely dictate. Would you like to hear it?

I opened my notebook to a blank page and prepared to copy it. Dictate it to me, I told him. Improve it, he said, and dictated.

To choose a book in the profusion of books. I stop at any one whatsoever and read a page I seem to remember. The last word continues with the first: When I reread the first word, time has already passed. I understand that this page multiplies a single phrase, that I continue as if I had recovered the time when I began. The whole book is made of that solitary phrase: Its unity is the same as its infinity. So nothing is perverted by memory. But soon the phrase that turns back on itself becomes a single word that proliferates on the page. The leaves of the book try to say the word in a rush. Time is bisyllabic and it affirms and denies. The word that fulfills the book, in the end, surpasses it. Now I am reading a single letter. I repeat it, resisting the expanding vertigo. Now its form abandons the book, opening my eyes. There is no one in the circle of that astonishment.

I reread what I had written and made, more or less, the following comments: If the circle of ink of a letter takes up the page and expands to where it exceeds the page, swallowing the reader, there would be no way to finish the fable. There would be nowhere to put the final period.

That's the point, he agreed, amused. The end must be thrown out. Now I will tell you the beginning. This fable, as you call it, was dictated to me by a dream. When I woke I knew I would record it later and I spoke outside the dream: "Father, why have you forsaken me?" To abruptly recite a famous quote, it doesn't make sense, does it?

Perhaps that was the phrase you were reading on the page in the dream, I exclaimed, not without renewed enthusiasm. I mean, the phrase that opened until it was a word, a letter, a void.

We are rushing headlong into allegory, he laughed, because we lack the words.

In the dream, you were the son, I continued, imperturbable; when you woke, you were then the father.

In that case, I would be an orphan, he said. One of those little heroes of Kipling who are adopted by the English language.

The father has died, I added, not the son. The dream speaks with inverted imagery. With anachronistic attributions, remember? It is the art of reading . . .

I've dreamt it, he reminded me, but you've written it down.

I'm not very sure of that, I joked. I don't have any other memorable quotation.

We're left with the wind, he remembered ironically. It passes right by and has no name.

It asks for the father, I responded, allegorically. It rereads the world, that Chinese encyclopedia.

In dreams, he sighed, the father is alive and he walks hand in hand with the son . . .

I was trying to call forward a quotation when a robust Texan lady and her adolescent son, weighed down with lyric and epic poetry, rushed toward our table with a triumphal cry.

Migrations

Monday morning walking down the hill toward the bus stop, I was expecting to see Charlie, but he was not there.

He had been there on Saturday morning when I took Kara to the children's reading hour at the bookstore. I had explained to my daughter that Charlie wakes up early for his morning drive. At the bus stop he greets each bus, inspects it, talks to the driver and, most often, decides to wait for the next bus.

His baggy clothes and loose hat, his large ears and broken speech make the driver smile, as if dealing with a child. The passengers avoid Charlie politely, but he recognizes me and, even if he does not address me directly, he raises his voice in my direction, and I acknowledge his stuttering news. At times Charley is already sitting on the bus quietly and as close as possible to the driver. It is clear that he is not going anywhere, just taking the whole round-trip along his favorite route.

But that Monday he was not around and, even if I had missed him before, his absence was more conspicuous this time. I have never seen him with a relative, but likely he lives in the vicinity with some family member. I stopped short of asking the driver.

Charlie was part of the human accidents of language, not part of us.

II

On my bus ride I was reading *The Frog,* John Hawkes' recent novel. Last week, having lunch with Jack at Adesso, he told me about the movie a couple of filmmakers were planning to make from his *The Blood Oranges.* Instead of the South of France, it would be shot in Mexico, in Cuernavaca, my hometown. I described the sunny, Mediterranean surroundings to him, the high white walks and radiant bougainvillea. Reading his new book, where a frog talks inside a child, I felt there were other voices; even the stories I used to read as a child. Jack's writing is woven of the same sweet fiber as those stories, and had evolved as memory itself. I know there is always another tale behind any reading; but I felt like walking into oblivion, alone and lost.

The next page soon carried me into an older story. I recognized Saint Paul's Cathedral, the poor children at its doors, skinny and dirty, begging and playing; and I thought how hard the characters had to work in those stories for middle-class readers. My question was, how much did these lengthy 19th century narratives of survival recovered real suffering?

Ferdinand de Saussure in his classes in Geneva at that time was discovering language's incapacity to depict reality. It is perhaps only fitting that his famous book was not written by him but compiled from his students' notes. Borges has written that a fact of life is only converted into language afterwards, as memory. If so, the present is not only elusive, it lacks a language of its own. Heraclitus's river flows in the reverberance of speech.

III

Marx and Fournier start their visions of a new world by speaking of children and their suffering and convert such rough force into the power of eloquence. Thanks to deduction and hyperbole, Marx and Fournier reshape time-present with the names of the future.

But I was not concerned with the nature of truth in one writer and the quality of vision in the other. My questions were moving in another direction. Was it possible to have a working plot without some didactic allegory? Why, in order to talk of suffering children, do I need to go back to Saint Paul's and Notre Dame? Wouldn't any story on today's children of migration be enough?

I couldn't answer these questions. I wrote a poem.

I wrote as I rode along in the bus, and my lines seemed to follow the straight road as well as the regular stops and sharp turns into downtown, while more passengers climbed in, among them vociferous high school kids, with their colorful dresses and bulky pants, and their black hair still wet. These students belonged not to Marx's first chapter but to Fourier's triumphant morning; they were full of their own force, laughing, mumbling and kidding. I wrote my first stanza in large letters, amused by the flow of words, moving ahead by the compulsion to answer a question, perhaps a rhetorical question.

These boys and girls are my story, I thought, but in what role or function? Most of them spoke high-pitched Spanish, and sometimes, on the bus, I have amused myself by deciphering their national accents. There are at least twenty different Spanish accents in Latin America, and I could identify some of them – the most obvious Argentinean,

Cuban, Mexican; the more recondite, perhaps Dominican or Guatemalan. But for these kids Spanish was already crossed with English. Maybe this was another language, not simply a mixture of Spanish and English but the jargon of Fourier's coming Hordes, the language of the first inhabitants of our new century – a physical affirmation of talking here, of being now.

I tried to go back to my poem but I was stopped by another question: How could I be sure of these teenagers' national origins? Was I using names of origin to give them a place instead, when it was clear that they were moving toward a new language? These boys and girls were the last product of migration, and perhaps both their speech and their ethnic origins were a force of meaning that was still evolving into language.

I was digressing in a domestic ride. I erased a couple of lines and started over.

This was my first poem in English. From time to time I feel the impulse to write a poem, most of the time half a poem, but always in Spanish. My English is merely Spanish making its way across the dubious sea of translation – that other migratory condition of the equivalence of naming.

IV

English, in this regard, is impeccable – it assumes that for each thing there is exactly one word, as if language were a true map of the world. Spanish is more tentative, and sometimes decorative. It allows us not one name but two, and even the possibility of over-naming, or re-naming. Anyhow, this need to say something (to say more is already a Spanish dilemma!), about my reading of *The Frog* between Charlie's stuttering and the voice of migrant children, had moved me into the muddy depths of language, with only my pen to find a way.

Carlos Fuentes once said that despite the fact he is totally bilingual (but is anybody completely bilingual?), he can only write in Spanish because for him it is only possible to make love and to dream in Spanish. That is, to be lost is perhaps only possible in Spanish. In other languages, one would believe you are in control of names and naming.

In any case, I was ready to risk writing this story in English precisely because I am not an accomplished bilingual. I love English iambic and some terse English prose. But I could never contribute to its poetic diction or its hard clarity. In Spanish, the vocalic sound of poetry can be both elemental and architectural; you believe you touch the sound, and that its fluidity is fletting.

Prose, on the other hand, can be ductile as a branch and it can reverberate like fire. Borges has said that English is a red language; Robert Graves, that the silvering sound of Spanish is closest to Latin.

My poem though was only a digression. I might call it "After Hawkes." It occurs to me now that one cannot exactly say that in Spanish. One needs to say, *"Después de leer a Hawkes."* And even so, you are not supposed to write poems after reading someone else; poetry in Spanish happens by chance but it is less devoted to everyday life. It is seen as a matter of inspiration. In writing poetry you move into another language – despite some demotic trends and the persuasions of speech. My poem, after all, fell between two languages too, but it didn't explore the English/Spanish borderlands.

It started as a matter-of-fact sort of poem, despite the reflexive mood. I have always admired the capacity of some major poets to write with other languages crossing their own in the opposite direction. It was the case of César Vallejo, in Paris, when he was composing his major poem on the Spanish Civil War. He wrote about the dead body of a militia-man: *"Su cadáver estaba lleno de mundo"* ("His cadaver was full of the world"), using a French idiom: *Plein de monde,* full of people, crowded. Another Peruvian, César Moro, the surrealist poet, wrote most of his work in French but with the freedom of a foreign speaker: Discovering associations of sound with a playful hand.

I sent the first version of my poem to Guy Davenport, who welcomed me into the English language, and had a suggestion: I should translate the poem into my own Spanish, and he would try to translate it into English. When I read Davenport's translation of Vicente Huidobro's famous poem on the Eiffel Tower, I felt that he has succeeded in creating a light English tower of words, a delicate weaving of vowels, probably taking into account the French model, the no less famous *calligramme* of the Eiffel Tower that Apollinaire erected with such childlike delight.

I was not capable of rewriting in Spanish a poem that I had already overwritten in English, much less when the poet and translator Alita Kelley, to my surprise, pointed to another sub-text: She discovered a bibliograpy of more or less recent French theoretical discourse as reference. Alita explained that she could read the Spanish behind my English, but that she couldn't follow the abstruse French! She also asked me to return the poem to Spanish, so she could translate it into

English. Suddenly, I had two translators of a poem that I still had not quite written. Like any good translator, Alita is always ready to turn her suggestions into a paper on the linguistic protocol of bilingual writing, and invited me to prove her point at the next conference of American translators. My poem in progress had already grown into a good example of the limits of writing in another language and the unlimited readings of such a futile enterprise. I think I know now how the mind of a translator works. My discovery does not involve the talents of a man or woman but the exchange processes of language itself. Some years ago, I helped my dear friend the Brazilian poet, Haroldo de Campos, translate a group of poems from Vallejo's most obscure book, *Trilce* (1922). Haroldo used to repeat José Lezama Lima's motto: "Only that which is difficult can be stimulant." He wanted to try the most impossible poems of that book, a book so obscure it is untranslatable even into its own Spanish language.

Then, I saw on the page a whole language in movement; I thought I saw a column of exchanging names; one word of the poem was rotating along the whole language; and I believe I saw the secret of a permanent substitution. The revelation or the fatigue proved that the locus of any name is a void, that any word is as good as another; but that only one word can have the value of the whole.

Yet even now I am not being faithful to the experience of working with Haroldo. I lose it at the very moment I attempt to fix it.

No less telling is the case of Gregory Rabassa, the great translator of *Cien años de soledad*. Greg becomes another person when he translates a book. To translate Luis Rafael Sánchez, he moved to Puerto Rico, and became a local. He has also been, many times, a Brazilian; but also Argentinean, and even Colombian. I am not saying that he becomes fully involved with the vernacular, but that he actually transforms himself into an eloquent native.

Was I writing my own translation now, or was I reluctantly exploring poetry in English? Was there, for the exiled writer, a space of migration, uncharted perhaps, formed by the crossing of languages? Was this notation another genre, simple marginalia, a sort of pretext, as good as any other, to keep talking about poetry? Was poetry the most difficult of all languages to reach, and were my friends and I engaged in a melancholic ritual around the lost poem and its improbable translation?

Too many questions for a handful of words.

V

Migrations

Children, I thought, had never worked so hard
as in the first chapter of Marx's *Das Capital.*
And I did not think of poverty
and indignation, nor of wasted children
at the doors of London (recovered
by Fourier as hordes migrating to a new world),
but of language, a garden of horror
larger than yours and mine

                         – as if children,
still without a discourse of their own,
should hold on to English (or for that matter, German),
to the hard edges of our master narratives.
And so the children of a lost city
illustrate a form of moral life,
its denial
                     – an epilogue to our reading.

The rest is reality,
the larger black sea of literal language.
And then I went down to a new border
to the Spanish steps of children crossing your page.

VI

Are suffering children translatable into the logic of language? Is the power of description enough to sustain life being lost in the cruelty of dispossession? Are these questions asking for a language capable of reshaping, if not reality, at least its borders? Perhaps to read is to move in the larger migration of meaning, asking for the children of language – those who will start again, anew.

It was a long trip. It started with Charlie.

I know now that he lacks a connecting language – the language of associations that Rosmarie Waldrop encountered between the early Spanish chronicles of the discovery and the discoveries of Alexander von Humboldt, the German traveler who wrote in French of his visit to the new Spanish-American shores. "There are no inferior races; all are destined equally to attain freedom," wrote Humboldt, who made of connecting the road to "humanization."

Charlie is unable to read, and he would not have made a good traveling companion for Baron von Humboldt. But he is my fellow-traveler, and I could tell him the story of a frog speaking inside a boy as the magic voice of a memory to which both of us belong.

Now I understand why he announces the names of the buses that arrive at our shore. He is waiting for his own story among the departing ships.

VII

Once in a conference at Brown, Jack Hawkes felt short
of words and turned to me, demanding the word he just lost.
"Plotting," I guessed and, happily, was right.
"I know so little Spanish that I am losing my English!"
he said, and we all laughed.

~ *Part II* ~

Blank Page

All day long this page has been the same in the
    beginning and in the end.

But do not regret such an illusion in the light of the
    yielding void.

You have closed that door and the street deviates now to
    another space revolving on the same promise.

Words that impose their rules on time.

Acts with a power that shapes their beginning with the
    footsteps of their end.

Fiction that you read in the page that never concedes
    its true name.

Translated by Amelia Simpson

Note on Returning

May devours these gardens very early and you have no peace
*

Back in Lima again, the wall predicts you
*

You would master in the name of terror, with mild eloquence
*

Where this prison ends you require a literal tree
*

Sick of doubt you reject its salty name
*

The city claims another victim and you won't regret it
*

There's a fire burning in the memory of an innocent animal
*

River that hastens the thirst of a younger winter
*

But what indistinct time was faithful here
*

The memory of its faith, you deserve that page
*

The law that measures an enemy time
*

You deserve that plight, some light.

Translated by Amelia Simpson

Port

1

Beside the sea I follow
its path of fever.
All the lights go out.

2

In the torrential
ambush of its names
I don't need to add another.

3

Now is when you are born
in the excess of the land
like the only thing clear.

4

Summer delivers
its stormy, candid head.
It recognizes my hand.

5

In the sand plaza there is
another sand:
the dream I travel through.

6

Longer than you
I walk over the fleeing
water that loses us.

7

Names of my country.
I owe them water and fire:
the language of praise.

8

Time is an animal
that harms every word.
But in the tempest
all the lights come back.

Translated by David Tipton

This Flute

You have made
this flute
from my bones –
         the voice

emerging
from the abyss
is clear –
         this

circular
guitar
is bloody –
         the drum

of a brave
heart
that dances
alone –
         the body

lost in the forest of
another body
is baroque.

Translated by James Hoggard

Time Passes

Time passes
and we follow –
          a drop
of water, its luster deceptive,
a syllable
without you –
          variations
of going,
today's changes
in yesterday,
tomorrow
we are already missing
this hour
without us –
          to steal
from time
handsful
of flowers
and shatter
their hope, but not
alone.

Translated by James Hoggard

The Angel

The
angel
also sings
the peace
of its passion
       Tyranny
of love
that gathers the
harvest
having given
to the tender earth
its fecund eye
       Its eyes are
the madonna's, the woman
who unbinds
my flesh
       She knows
the wet grass
under the May sun
the north the night
a divided fruit
       And she
chose you
in the forest of her dream
where I opened
the door.

Translated by James Hoggard

Interchangeable Sun

Savage summer sun
My current Keeper
Set my blood on fire, this
Saliva of yours:
Another
Of your earthly powers, I am
Interchangeable
With your life
When I have gone around
Under your thin gold
Like a rude bird
That burns
While the earth dissolves
Beside a woman floating
Full length on this blood
At your feet
We sleep like indolent gods
In your unfinished creation

Translated by Forrest Gander

Song of the Mother Language

Why in the total diversity
of which we're this part
are we not all
under the cloudy night
that drifts over reddish
like a smooth partition
dissolving in the distance
and increasing the time
of the dinner for two,
deducted by the fathers,
eyes that met
in an entirely different idea
that waits for us to finish
this phrase echoing
with the sound of their voices,
the light that makes us
children, newlyweds,
when we drink and eat
what's been given us,
that totally measly trifle
in which we need
those we're far from,
relatives who deserve
this desert's bread.

Translated by James Hoggard

Knowing We Might Still Return

Knowing we might still return
awakens some
tender organ within us – enough evidence
that we are moved, almost at peace with ourselves.
We are nurtured
on a milk not of the body,
we are the warm, tender orphans
who inspire a rush of mother-love.
News spreads of flooding
along the borders.
Traces of mud betray our flight.
Homesickness worthy of epic
makes us swear allegiance
to our lost land – amid torn banners.
Our faces are daubed with tribal truths.
Such is the irony of those who still believe
in their strength, it is the fist
hammering on the silent door.
We, the uprooted, awakened by the surge
that takes our breath away.

Translated by Alita Kelley

Emotions, III

This summer of '91
Hurricane Bob whipped the shores
of Rhode Island. Its romantic fury
made my house tremble.
And I saw a tree on the hill snap
under the power of the wind
like a biblical quotation.
With tragic clamor, dramatic rather,
it carried off from a green paradise
the new family of the red flamboyant tree.
I was frightened.
Not for myself but for a revelation.
Nature by chance
of its broken force mixed contrary materials
and erased what we call kingdoms
(a balance of classical chaos).
We are I said to myself these makings of Fortune.
An image tamed like a fistful
of reality stolen from the wind.
At the edge of the wild river
this metaphorical excess was able
to save my life.

Translated by Clementine Rabassa

Emotions, V

Its sweet symbolic animal
changes in name and
flees from the place of speech.
A native figure, almost maternal,
decorated with grape leaves and
chrysanthemums, somewhat Pompeian
at the time for distinguishing
between the virtues of the volute.
Promises of civilization of sign
and yearning, the seduction
of a flight contemplated
on the anonymous frontier.
Because between feeling and saying
there is no other complicity
than this desire proposed
as a conspiracy.
Anyway, the sweet
symbolic animal flees
beyond the woods,
where hunting has
yet to give it a name.

Translated by Clementine Rabassa

Emotions, XII

After a sluggish day at the beach
I wouldn't want to write another poem: after
the sun and water their names should be enough.
But one ends up describing as fortuitous
that coincidence of what's sharp, the virtue
of what's bright, facing the iodized breeze,
in the azure variation of the morning.
Closing my eyes among the crowd
that thirsts for light.
After a sherry on the terrace
we abandon the tribe of bathers,
who prefer the hottest part of midday.
For an instant, the radiance of color lulls
language to sleep cutting it loose from its moorings,
as if it were no longer indebted to objects
and much less to my contemporaries.
Many things, few names.
And we go off to recover speech, filled
with a primary silence,
between a miracle and the middle class.

Translated by Clementine Rabassa

Emotions, XIV

I am flying to Atlanta today the 14th of February
thinking that life is an anonymous
labor of mixed style, detailed and
exempt from the slowness of a theme.
This is an imaginary symmetry
imposed by the need for articulation,
correlatives of a theoretical field
where the shades of form and color
are bound and untied.
I'd be the last to deny the pleasure
of this flexibility: the undaunted courage
of the body, the instructive
wisdom of its hands
and its well of honey.
By all means let's agree that this is
a long repeated trial: the moment
lacks history
but the language is more suited
to discourse than to exaltation.
The dance is more pure
in the ecstasy that conquers it.
It's a way of saying
almost believing
so as not to abandon the dance.

Translated by Clementine Rabassa

Emotions, XIX

What we have left is the letter: life
in its own alphabet,
where the day is measured
syllabically, as if the future were
a spelling bee.
A pure past, its speech consists
of those places made mutual by oblivion.
Forget it all but the Baroque
dedicated to the nickname.
There is nothing to remember about the
Heraclitan river that flowed along,
just the redundancy.
Illusions of the proper noun
when split in two the word
leaves a residue of syllables,
handwriting without a signature.
The syllable, Sibyl,
speaks all languages.
It is illiterate only about the future,
which we write tentatively
as if we clipped it
letter by letter.
ABC of a language
disappeared.

Translated by Clementine Rabassa

Self-Portrait in Toledo

To be this shadow
of El Greco, these eyes, these
lips, this illusion that death
stops at this reposing black,
free of light that
spoils the idea of eternity: golden
is the evanescent matter
that perpetuates us.

    I am not
this shadow but this flame
of El Greco, this yearning for
the eternal
freed by death,
these pale ochers burning
in the glance that carries
the final passionate order
of the world.

    To be that
trembling of his hand, that
line groping through a tortured
sky as if the body
would never know time,
the journey that turns
madness into a model
of reason, for the sake of faith,
this scarcely human business
that busies the powers
sketched in the ritual of miracle:

the taciturn body, the sheer pain
of an unbelieving world.

     Nor are you
this river or stone
burning like a torch
of time: desire's monument,
stretched out in the abyss
of its own building,
when knights have given life
and tremble with
eternity. What being
but this paradox,
like a mockery, this wonder.

     You are not
dust or nothingness: the glance you are
that kindles El Greco's eyes
over his own grave opened
for whoever peers
beneath the only miracle: to no longer
be here but simply be
someone who sees,
seeing the hand that controls
its own burial
the way the singular power
of the open eye controls the closed.

     We are
so much exaltation, so much tormented
blue and tortuous gray:
the meeting of the body
and its treasure, each vulnerable
to the other, creatures

of flesh and question,
in the unpeopled scene
where we wake alone.

      We are no longer
this speech, we are its contradiction,
the emblems silence us and there are no
more hands to carry us
to paradise: alone among ruins,
we are the repetitions of ritual,
naked in our speaking
as in our death:
the body alone remains
like the final form
of lost speech.

      Many towers
high walls say too much
and tell us too little:
their history is not their ruin:
it is their prophecy
of resisting, as in an El Greco,
everything human
under the skies.
Under the skies you
are no longer merely history,
that tourist guide
babbling English,
you are the sure promise
that time once again
will conquer stone:
beneath hands in the form
of a bursting star.

You are
this Moorish dome, this inscribed
steel of Mudejar stone,
this spreading tree
of origins:
burnt architecture
in the baroque eye
of the returning adventurer
who jolts you awake
like the wonder that occupies
those who are still searching
outside time – in sense.

And kings
fell to their graves
for the sake of eternity:
tourists taking pictures
of metamorphic stone
only add another to the hoard
of fleeting images, but you,
for the sake of history,
you will feel the traces
of an empire that artisans buried
beneath their writing:
doors, domes, arches,
-how much burying time needs!
to the line add
this passion of design.

And art
is the shape of the fleeting: its miracle
is not to resist, is to have
given to passion's themes
the sense of design that only fails

after incarnating time in work.
To feel this Plateresque ash
is to see the crowded plaza
praising the height of inscribed stone:
people tasting the very water,
this image where an irreparable
time is portrayed,
that rippling.

    I know more of myself
in this river or stone
more of you, being or not,
seeing the knight's face
or artisan's hands,
the painter's stroke,
the sign of the master inscribed
in this image of a world
as lost as any while I sustain
my world and yours
in this abyss of eternity
where time
is engraved for me: whoever you are
peering between the stone and the mirage.

Translated by James Houlihan

About the Author

Julio Ortega (Peru, 1942) is numbered among the most profound contemporary critics of Latin American literature. Formerly a professor at the University of Texas at Austin and Brandeis University, he has taught Latin American literature at Brown University since 1989. His poetry, fiction, and drama have received prizes in Lima, Madrid, Paris and Mallorca. His creative work has been translated into English, French, Italian, German, and Russian, as well as Quechua and Farsi. His fiction includes *La mesa del padre* (1995), *Ayacucho, Good Bye* (1994), and *Canto de hablar materno* (1992). His work has appeared in *Antaeus, London Magazine, The Michigan Review, The Boston Globe Magazine, Agni,* among other journals. His literary criticism includes *Poetics of Change: The New Latin American Narrative* (1986), *Garcia Márquez and the Powers of Fiction* (1988), and *Arte de innovar* (1994). With Carlos Fuentes, he edited *The Picador Book of Latin American Short Stories* (1998) and *The Vintage Book of Latin American Stories* (2005). His most recent book is *Transatlantic Translations: Dialogues in Latin American Literature* (London, 2006).

Acknowledgments

"Las Papas," first appeared in the Boston Globe's *Magazine,* 1988; also in *Sudden Fiction International,* Robert Shapard and James Thomas, eds. (Norton, 1989). "The Incomplete Work of Edward Garatea" and "A Poem by Edward Garatea" first appeared in *World Literature Today,* Summer 1994; "The Art of Reading" in *Antaeus,* Spring 1993; "Syllables and Lines" in the *Anthology of Contemporary Latin American Literature, 1960-1984,* Barry J. Luby and Wayne H. Finke, eds. (Farleigh Dickinson University Press, 1986); "On the Birth of Love" in *Tamaqua,* Fall 1992; "Inter-changeable Sun" in *Tamaqua,* Spring 1993; "Self Portrait in Toledo" in *Café Solo,* Vol. 5, Nos. 3-4, 1987; and the "Emotions" series, from the chapbook, *Emotions* (Merrick, NY: Cross Cultural Communications, 1999).

Colophon

This first edition of *The Art of Reading: Stories and Poems*, by Julio Ortega, has been printed on 70 pound non-acidic paper containing fifty percent recycled fiber. Text and poem titles have been set using Adobe Caslon type; story titles in Parisian ICG type. The first 50 signature sets to be pulled from the press have been numbered and signed by the author. Wings Press books are designed by Bryce Milligan.

Wings Press was founded in 1975 by Joanie Whitebird and Joseph F. Lomax, both deceased, as "an informal association of artists and cultural mythologists dedicated to the preservation of the literature of the nation of Texas." The publisher/editor since 1995, Bryce Milligan is honored to carry on and expand that mission to include the finest in American writing, without commercial considerations clouding the choice to publish or not to publish. We know well that writing is a transformational art form capable of changing the world, primarily by allowing us to glimpse something of each other's souls. Good writing is innovative, insightful, and interesting. But most of all it is honest. In a similar spirit, Wings Press is committed to treating the planet itself as a partner. Thus we use as much recycled material as possible, from the paper on which the books are printed to the boxes in which they are shipped.

Editor of the present volume, Robert Bonazzi, is also an old hand in the small press world, long the publisher / editor of Latitudes Press (1966-2000). Bonazzi and Milligan share a commitment to independent publishing and have collaborated on numerous projects over the past 25 years. As Robert Dana wrote in *Against the Grain*, "Small press publishing is personal publishing. In essence, it's a matter of personal vision, personal taste and courage, and personal friendships." Welcome to our world.

Wings Press titles are distributed to the trade by
The Independent Publishers Group • www.ipgbook.com